Living in the past (and present)

Creative writing inspired by archives

Southampton Creative Histories Group

ACKNOWLEDGEMENTS

We would like to thank:
Southampton City Libraries and their helpful staff for the use of the wonderful Seminar Room, and the many ways in which they have supported our group. Special thanks to the lovely people in Local Studies, who never failed to find stimulating materials to inspire our writing.
We would like to thank the artist Mr Sean Lynch for providing the photograph of the water jug that was on display at his exhibition, A Murmur repeated, that was held in Southampton.

Photo credits:

Water jug	Sean Lynch
Holyrood church	Peter Nicol-Harper
War memorial	Val Claisse
Hollybrook Children's Home	Southampton Heritage Photographs
Tudor House	Peter Nicol-Harper
Air raid	Judy Theobald
Library memorial	Peter Nicol-Harper
Netley Hospital	Southampton Heritage Photographs
Romany children	Southampton Heritage Photographs
Windrush memorial	Susy Churchill
Writing in the time of COVID	David Burnett
Cover design:	Susy Churchill

Living in the past (and present)

Contents

Living in the past (and present)

Living in the past (and present)

Introduction

Autumn Term 2019
At the start of the autumn term our Southampton Hidden Histories Writing Group had so enjoyed working with Nazneen Ahmed as our writer-in-residence at the Central Library that when she was unable to continue we decided to see if we could "go it alone". The fact that we have been able to carry on writing and produce this anthology shows how well she gave us the confidence to do so. We dedicate this anthology to her.

It was during this term that we decided on the themes on which we would like to write. We continued the tradition of visiting local places for inspiration. Our first was the John Hansard Gallery.

The publicity about the Windrush Scandal then gave us an unplanned theme.

Spring Term 2020
January: New Year, and that felt relevant for the three key themes we had identified for our work this year: Fresh Starts, the Working World, and Neighbourhoods. We had a plan, and visits we intended to make. We started by exploring the historical development of some of the different neighbourhoods that make up the city of Southampton, courtesy of materials provided by the Local Studies team.

Vintage copies of the Southern Daily Echo during the war years led to a deeper investigation of this theme. A visit to the Solent Sky Museum, and the newspaper photograph of a wedding taking place amongst the rubble of a bombed-out church stimulated us all.

Then came coronavirus, and lockdown - the Library was closed. Hastily, we decided to continue via video-conferencing - which gave us a peek into each other's working spaces!

Summer Term

Amidst the worrying challenges that the pandemic and the lockdown brought to our daily lives, the writers continued to meet via Zoom and relied on the internet resources for research.

During the summer term, the writers began to reflect on the Travellers and the Romany community and how they had shaped the history and demography of the city of Southampton and the effects of their varying extent of assimilation into it.

The writing exercises, that were outside the usual historical theme have been an instant success and those made us think laterally, and express our feelings artistically. Besides, they have been fun!

The pandemic caused by Covid-19 virus has been altering the entire globe in an unimaginable manner and the group decided unanimously to consider the novel experience as a writing inspiration. Sometimes, stresses in life unearth hidden creativity! Fresh with extraordinary experiences and a cocktail of emotions, words flowed out naturally, without constraints.

Visits

Sometimes, one's writing muse awakes at the most unexpected times, when not even a pencil or a piece of paper is within one's reach. Here are the experiences of our writers who made personal visits to events, exhibitions and museums in the Southampton area and saw their surroundings in a different perspective.

Living in the past (and present)

The Water Jug on Display

A cracked, glued, imperfect relic
an asymmetric jug on display
like gem-encrusted earthenware

Whose fingers had slipped around
the lopsided handle to tip water?
a subservient peasant wife

a herb brewing witch healer
a Benedictine nun in black
or a butler in the hall of a manor

Why did the potter etch two hands?
Was it a pictogram of his endurance
or the sad tale of their love?

His and her hands lay side by side
ready to tangle. But in adversity
they had to remain still to eternity

Born from dust the jug survived
to repeat the murmur of the potter
the customer and the life now in dust

In a congregation, what will the jug
tell to its progeny,
the slick machine made clones?

Champika Wijayaweera

*Inspired by the Water Jug on Display at the Exhibition of Sean
Lynch's "A Murmur Repeated" that was held in John Hansard
Gallery, Southampton from 20th July to 28th September 2019*

Living in the past (and present)

Paratrooper

He didn't join with comrades old:
The veterans, military or the young.
But rather shunned those solemn crowds.

Standing apart and at a distance
Leaning lightly against a tree
A bulldog at his feet
He wore his memories privately and alone.

Last post still echoing in the morning air
This "red beret" man
Medals and hat badge glinting in the sun
Stole noiselessly away.

Ready for anything.
Utrinque Paratus.

Val Claisse

(Observed at the Remembrance Day service 2019 in Netley Abbey)

Women's Work

Gran was a series of rolls, that rippled in turn when she laughed, going up from her comfortable tummy and ending with her double chin – and she laughed often.
She was a pair of clever hands that made things: rock cakes, clothes for dollies, school cardigans when I wanted an anonymous garment, bought at the shop like everyone else. Gran taught me to knit and sew, crochet and bake, and heard my adolescent heartbreak without interrupting.
She enjoyed Barbara Cartland stories, sported glittery cardigans, and wore lipstick till the day before she died.

It was after her death that I discovered Ada: born at the turn of the century, the outbreak of war spared her from the predicted future in domestic service. There is a photo of her in a boiler suit, tiny waist and generous hips, her hair bundled into a bonnet. But the top buttons are undone, turned down to lapels, and she sports brogues with heels, tied with ribbon bows. She gazes directly into the camera: this was no modest miss who would give a 'yes, ma'am, no ma'am' to a middle-class housewife. Did she resent having to give up her independence when the war ended and returning soldiers wanted their jobs back?

She married in 1919, and my uncle was born in 1920, followed by my mother two years later. It was when I was twenty, dating an unsuitable guy on the rebound, that Mum told me her parents did not have a happy marriage: Ada's childhood sweetheart died in the first months of the war, and the man she married was 'nervy'. I have only the haziest memory of Grandad: a figure in the shed at the end of the garden. I learned that she worked as a 'clippie' – a bus conductor – to supplement the family income. Grandad was often out of work, his shakes proving too much of a hindrance to many employers.

Living in the past (and present)

But they had four children, and went to the dances at the Club
every Friday night.

In her sewing box, a collection of corsages in different colours:
strips of organza sewn into the semblance of flowers. Did she
learn to make these from a magazine, or were they her own
invention? I found lacy shawls, crocheted from the finest of yarn,
in ivory, gold, pink, baby blue, neatly folded in her wardrobe
drawer, and imagine a dance dress, created from her wedding
gown, bedecked with a corsage in a colour to complement the
shawl. Those clever hands, constantly busy with 'women's
work'.

Susy Churchill

*Inspired by an embroidery at the Gathered Memories Exhibition in
Southampton Central Library*

A wedding among the rubble

We visited the Solent Sky Museum, which houses an excellent display of old black and white photographs of wartime Southampton and the 1940 'Blitz.'
One photograph of a wedding ceremony being conducted in the ruins of Holyrood church really captured our imaginations and the resulting creative - and entirely fictional - accounts reinvent the wedding party and their guests' memories of that day.

Holyrood church 2020

Behind the lens

They say that the camera never lies and I fear that this is no exception - there is no truth being hidden here. The camera clearly shows that this couple's marriage will soon be as wrecked as the rubble that is now Holyrood Church. Not even their families look happy about this union, so I am guessing that it is not their parents' wishes that these two should be married. War does strange things to people - maybe it was this couple's fear that they may not be here tomorrow that has resulted in them swearing to be together until death us do part. Maybe it all started at a dance one night, a look across the crowded dance floor and the urge to discover sex before a bomb sent them to kingdom come. Only that urge has now led to the stork being on his way and their parents forcing them down the aisle.

When I was asked to photograph this supposed happy occasion, I thought that it would help take my mind away from the horrors of war and bomb damaged streets of Southampton. The opposite is far from it.

It takes me back to my wedding day back on 4th August 1916 but not because me and my dear Sarah were unhappy - far from it in fact. In the short time we had together things were good until the Spanish Flu got her.

But I'll always remember the first time I saw our wedding photo when she sent me one whilst I was lying in a hospital bed somewhere in Belgium and I remember thinking that despite my smile, I could see utter sadness in my eyes. Not because of Sarah but because I was due back at the front in a few hours and all I could think, standing outside the church listening to everyone's cheers, was that I did not want to go back. I didn't want to go back to the mud, blood and destruction, I wanted to stay in Blighty with my dear Sarah and not have to worry that I

Living in the past (and present)

may not see another sunset. It was lying there in that small hospital bed that I realised that the camera never lies.

Becky Sharp

Canon Merry's epithalamion

"DEARLY beloved, we are gathered together here in the sight of God, and in the face of this Congregation, to join together this man and this woman in holy Matrimony; which is an honourable estate, instituted of God in the time of man's innocency,"
So hard to remember a time of innocence – before fire rained from the sky, and an Austrian demagogue poured tanks across his every border. Are you still in sight, God? When the Luftwaffe seem to be targeting our churches are they attacking you as well as us?

"the mystical union that is betwixt Christ and his Church;"
And the Church is so much more than its buildings – but it hurts to see so much destruction – and I never thought to solemnize a marriage surrounded by rubble.

"first miracle that he wrought, in Cana of Galilee;"
I imbibed too freely yesterday – drunkenness is not appropriate for an ordained minister, and I will not repeat that state. But my nerves were rattled – and only my dear Catherine witnessed my loose tongue and anger.

"is not by any to be enterprised, nor taken in hand, unadvisedly, lightly, or wantonly, to satisfy men's carnal lusts and appetites,"
He looks pretty lusty, the bridegroom, but he'll be off on active service soon, I gather. It doesn't feel right to be making a marriage when I've only just met the groom, but such is the pressure of war. She doesn't look happy, young Violet – not the radiant bride we were expecting. Is she just upset because her beautiful dress is framed by rubble and shattered windows? Dad looks glum, too.
Oh, how could I have forgotten! That fourth whisky last night! Poor Violet – to lose her grandmother, in such a tragic fashion, and so close to her wedding day. Did Mother have time to prepare her for her wedding night? She is an innocent, young Violet – not like so

many of the others here. I'm sure half of them have dallied, up on the Common.

"First, it was ordained for the procreation of children,"
Is it wise to bring children into a world like this? But I married my Catherine while on leave from the trenches – and we did so, choosing to believe in a better future.

"Secondly, it was ordained for a remedy against sin, and to avoid fornication; that such persons as have not the gift of continency might marry,"
Seems as if precious few nowadays are willing to avoid fornication – but I remember the urgency of 'live today, for tomorrow we may die'. Why do we keep falling into war? This Hitler is a bully, and must be stopped – and diplomacy has failed … but do we have to keep sending off a whole generation of young men to be killed or maimed?

"If any man can shew any just cause, why they may not lawfully be joined together, let him now speak, or else hereafter for ever hold his peace."
It's so irreverent, but every time I say these words, I picture a Laurel and Hardy scene, with some random person piping up from the congregation, then another person popping up and the pair having a silly argument!

"Wilt thou love her, comfort her, honour, and keep her, in sickness and in health; and, forsaking all other, keep thee only unto her, so long as ye both shall live?"
And how long will that be? Violet is as much at risk as her Arthur while these bombs rain down around us.

"Wilt thou obey him, and serve him, love, honour, and keep him?"
Modern women seem less inclined to obey their husbands. But when they're being called to work building aeroplanes and such like, I suppose they might feel they are as strong as men?

"Who giveth this woman to be married to this man?"
I've never seen poor Norman looking so anxious – we're all rattled by the air raids, but he looks haunted. Does he really support this marriage? It's so hard to hand your daughter over to some lusty chap, remembering your own urges at that age.

"Those whom God hath joined together let no man put asunder."
But, sadly, Hitler's troops will destroy the marriages I make … perhaps we should pray that they both live long enough to encounter the ordinary difficulties that strengthen the bonds of wedlock.

"I pronounce that they be man and wife together, In the Name of the Father, and of the Son, and of the Holy Ghost. Amen."
For as long as it may be. Where are you, Lord, in this time of turmoil?

"As it was in the beginning, is now, and ever shall be: world without end."
And, through the ages, other ministers have struggled to see your grace in the face of Man's inhumanity to Man.

"This woman may be loving and amiable, faithful and obedient to her husband; and in all quietness, sobriety, and peace, be a follower of holy and godly matrons."
Though young brides have ever sought to establish their own household, according to their own whims - and those who should be setting a godly example are curling their hair and fretting about shortages of their cosmetics!

"ALL ye that are married, or that intend to take the holy estate of Matrimony upon you, hear what the holy Scripture doth say as touching the duty of husbands towards their wives, and wives towards their husbands."
And I must remind myself not to take my dear Catherine for granted, and to show her more care – for she takes better care of me, than I do of her.

Living in the past (and present)

"Wives, submit yourselves unto your own husbands, as unto
the Lord. For the husband is the head of the wife,"
*But is it heretical of me to wonder sometimes whether we would live
a holier life if wives had the running of households and nations – for
it seems to me that it is men who crave and provoke wars...*

Susy Churchill

Freddie's Story

Vi promised she would write every day. I hoped for a letter
from her, day after relentless day, but nothing arrived. I was
beginning to think she'd changed her mind so I decided to write
first and ask her to put me out of my misery, once and for all.
My heart nearly missed a beat when a letter arrived but it was
from Mum not Vi and she dropped the bombshell that Vi was to
be married after Christmas, to that jerk, Arthur - I couldn't
believe what I was reading, it was like a dagger had been stuck
into me.

I was due a 48 hour pass so jumped at the chance to get back
home and try to meet Vi. I knew she didn't love Arthur and I
also knew what a womaniser he was. He would lead her one
hell of a dance if she married him. If I could just look her full in
the eyes I would have my answer.

It was 2 a.m. on the 3rd when I finally made it into Southampton
and risking the blackout wardens made my way to Vi's home on
Methuen Street. I threw some gravel at her window until at last
she opened it. Moments later she was outside with me and
searching her face I had my answer.

Then she was begging me to take her away and between her
sobs I got the whole picture about her father catching Arthur
with his hand up her skirt and his insistence then that he must
marry her.
'Hey, slow down Vi, I love you, you must know that.'
'But you never wrote and when I knew I was pregnant I was
scared and I thought Dad would turn me out if he knew. I
thought you had forgotten me. Oh! it is such a mess. The baby
is yours, Freddie, and could only be yours.'

I felt as if the air had been knocked out of my body. I drew Vi to
me and promised to find a way.

Living in the past (and present)

So here I am in bombed out Holyrood church waiting my chance, as agreed with Vi, to speak up when the minister calls out for anyone who knows of any impediment....but then just as he reaches that moment two onlookers are taking a photograph and that is where you find us today, locked in a second of time, with no future.

'Tear up that photograph and set us free to live our future, please.'

Val Claisse

Normann, the Father of the Bride

Sleeping with the enemy didn't do me any harm.

Here I am at the Solent Himmel Museum already regretting my cheapskate decision to only pay ten deutschmarks because, of course, the place is packed with sub human frauleins. I've come to enjoy the recorded roar of the V4 rocket recently on display, but I'm distracted by one group of what appears to be all women, stupid enough to be breaking the law by talking in English in a public place. They obviously don't realize that I'm bi-lingual. I ease myself alongside the one called Petra, trying to ignore her cheap English perfume. They switch to speaking in the universal tongue. They are going to write fiction about a Greatest War Wedding photograph. I peer over the good looking one's shoulder. I am stunned to see that it is none other than that of my daughter's wedding!

I have never been so furious in all my long life. I could feel bile rising up in my throat. Fortunately, I was right next to the rathskeller, so I ordered half a stein of Becks and a currywurst and took out my pocket book of Rainer Maria Rilke and read my favourite of his Sonnets to Orpheus to calm me down. Now let me explain...

I thought I, not just a Blackshirt, but also a German spy, was a dead duck, when that MI5 officer turned up at my daughter's wedding. Fortunately, the V3 Mark 2 rockets quickly changed everything. After the Reich's glorious victory I discovered that the experiments on the live underclass at the Kaiser Adolf Military Hospital in Netley had led to a breakthrough in prolonging the lives of the Master Race. I volunteered for the first trials. Unfortunately for the 3rd Reich, which will certainly last for at least a thousand years, the success rate was only one percent, but here I am 80 years later still looking the same as I did in that photograph. I wonder that the obviously most intelligent of them didn't comment on the coincidence. Thinking about that photo, I reckon that the dear old Canon might have been the only one there who thought that my Violet was a white wedding virgin. At least our dear departed Fuhrer put an end to all that immoral ungodly behaviour. It's not so good anymore under Empress Merkel.

You think I'm so upset, because I hate the idea of those sub humans having the audacity to fictionalise me and my family and friends. No! The truth is that the press photographer took many more than just the one that the Hampshire Advertiser published. I'd bought all the photos myself. My daughter's wedding was a joyous occasion. That published photo was taken just as Canon Merry said "Let him now speak, or else hereafter for ever hold his peace". I wasn't the only one on tenterhooks at that moment, what with my best friend Nick being there. Yes, I did know what he'd been up to with my daughter and then that Freddie turning up at the last minute.

Now I would like to end by saying all the other photos show everyone smiling happily. So, you see photographs are deceptive and the camera can lie.

Peter Nicol-Harper

Sylvia smiled

Smile for the photographer! Don't want to be preserved for posterity with a face like thunder ...

Norman said it was my smile that first intrigued him: 'Mona Lisa' he called me when we met back in Serbia at the start of the Great War – the 'First World War' they're calling it now – how many are the blighters planning? One every generation to reduce population size? Keep the plebs' numbers down to prevent the revolution?

Hard to believe how I fell for Norman – he was a dashing figure, and so useful around the camp – really interested in all the vehicles – and he did help me keep the ambulance running. The armoured cars were what really fascinated him, of course, but then he was an engineer. And I was enchanted that he loved poetry.

Is he actually Serbian? He claimed to be, back then, but his support for Mosley's blackshirts makes me wonder... I only knew a few phrases, and he never seemed to be around when other Serbian nationals were chattering away. His injury was real enough – you can't fake wounds! I was only an ambulance driver, not a proper nurse, but I saw enough broken bones to recognise one. What are you thinking, Sylvia? Why on earth would he pretend to be something he's not?

But then again, I've done my fair share of pretending...

Oh, Violet! I hope your marriage proves more successful than your mother's – but wartime weddings don't have a great future. She's been so tight-lipped since I got back – of course, this bombsite isn't what she dreamed of when she planned her wedding. She never seemed that interested in Arthur when he first joined Norman as an apprentice, but people do change. What isn't she telling me?

Of course, I haven't exactly been the perfect mother. My love for Norman had vanished before she was even born, but you make the best of things. Thank you, Mother, for your words of wisdom: "You made the bed, so you must lie in it!" I've lied, all right! You were more help to me when you went doolally than you ever were when you had all your marbles: gave me the perfect reason to leave the marital home to 'go and look after you'. Vi was fourteen by then, and happy enough to look after the house.

If only I hadn't followed my childhood sweetheart Edgar to Serbia – seemed like an adventure, and I fancied myself a heroine. Driving ambulances to the front line was scary, though it gave me the chance to discover what I could do. Edgar was much less attractive when I saw him surrounded by volunteers of all nationalities, and I separated myself from him as gently as I could. Norman was really good looking, in that Slavic way, and he paid attention to me, seemed fascinated about my life: so much more exciting than Edgar. That was then: now he's just a bad-tempered bully, and wicked when he's had a drink.

But if I hadn't gone to Serbia, I'd never have met Steven. Strange that we didn't click at first. It was at that reunion in 1924 that I fell for him. Norman had refused to go, but Mother agreed to look after the girls, and I flounced off on my own. Darling Steven, so modest: thought I was out of his reach. Sixteen years now. He comments on my smile, too.

How are we going to carry on seeing each other, now that Mother is gone? I could just bite the bullet, and let Norman divorce me – I'm sure he suspects. I suppose I could volunteer for war work – I still know how to drive, and I'm sure they'll need people willing to drive ambulances in this war, too. That would give me plenty of reasons to stay away for weeks at a time.

Best of luck, Violet – maybe, one day, we can have a real mother-daughter chat? Share our secrets, and smile at the compromises we've made?

Susy Churchill

The camera never lies

Well, who would have thought that on Tuesday 3ʳᵈ of December 1940 yours truly, Raymond Rogers, would be shivering in a roofless, stained glass windowless bombed out Holyrood church as best man for a bridegroom that I'd never met before? You want to know more? Well pin back your lugholes…
You'll remember that Saturday November 30ᵗʰ was the weekend of the Southampton blitz?
All of us army types were ordered from the parade ground into the air raid shelters when the sirens went off. At roll-call a certain Private Ivor Walker was missing, but we initially thought nothing of it, as a bit of AWOL happens all the time. Turns out he was more interested in visiting his tart, Juicy Lucy, in Derby Road. Again, that was no big deal, except that a bomb takes off the roof and the front of the house and there he is in bed face down starkers from the waist down stone cold dead. She's unconscious underneath him. The ARP blokes spread the word and we all had a good laff. "Lucky bugger. What a way to go. He was only doing his duty, whilst she was thinking of England. He'll get a posthumous medal for dying on active service etc."
So far so good, until my Sergeant tells me that this bloke in our regiment is getting married and Ivor was the best man and that I've drawn the shortest straw and I'm ordered to be the best man. Well you could have knocked me down with a feather.
To tell you the truth I've never been successful yet with girls. For some reason they keep giving me the heave-ho. But then, I'm introduced to the bridesmaid Betty Something at the "Fox and Grapes" before the big event. After a drink I corner her outside the toilets and suggest that the best man and the bridesmaid follow tradition and have a bit of "Slap and Tickle". I get a slap, but no tickle. I realize that she's up herself, the snooty bitch. I bet she grew up in Upper Shirley or somewhere like it.
Then to make matters worse it's muggins who ends up having to shovel away the rubble from the aisle before the bride can

enter. Now things are beginning to look up because Vi has only her wedding dress on even though it's freezing and she's clearly not wearing a brassiere if you see what I mean?

I've taken an instant dislike to the groom, a Mr Arthur C. Clarke if you please. How come he gets a girl down the aisle? Of course, he's a rich bastard. I bet just from looking at the father of the bride that he's the sort who insists on no sex without a wedding ring. And I'm sure that he's going to try and give her a baby tonight, a boy, of course, in case he doesn't last through to the end of this bloody war.

The vicar bloke must be used to this sort of thing, because he gave me a little book which tells me what the best man should do and say, including jokes in my speech which are bloody acceptable! The only thing that I'm looking forward to is to get my hands on the bride. At the reception back at the pub she and the groom danced cheek to cheek to 'Moonlight Serenade'. I thought that the best man might have the second dance with the bride. It was 'In the Mood' and I thought "Well I am, so here goes". But no! Just as I'm advancing on her, the groom grabs me and snarls "My wife doesn't dance with strangers." I'm tempted to deck him, but he's bigger than me. I just turn away and I'm about to walk out to go to see if I've got enough money to finally pop my cherry with Juicy Lucy when lo and behold for some reason the bridesmaid comes over to me all smiles and says "Let's dance," and I think "This could be my lucky night."

Peter Nicol-Harper

Thoughts of the Laughing Lady

Congratulations, Vi! From the bottom of my heart, I'm happy for you, dear. To me, your wedding is the happiest event in this sombre period.

When you first told me that you were going out with Arthur, I admit, I was hurt, because I broke up with him only a fortnight before that. (I should have known better - Arthur would never allow grass to grow under his feet!)

"I may or may not return. I still haven't flavoured the intimacy of love," he begged repeatedly. Yes, we live in desperate times and every minute counts. Any moment, they could send his regiment abroad, and I was scared to take risks and travel along the same path where mom had lumbered two decades ago. I haven't seen my Dad, and making everything worse, he hadn't had an opportunity to discover about me. Mom had given in to his request, just once.

The following week his regiment had been shipped to foreign lands. Even before she had missed her menses, she had learned he had been killed in action. My grandparents, archetypes of that era, had shut the door to Mom and unborn me. Fortunately, Mom's godmother, a childless war-widow of the Boer War, had opened the door to her. So, I was born and grew up in Southampton, miles away from Yorkshire. I have never met my relatives and have no intention of doing so.

Fortunately, the last war had opened many opportunities for women, but it wasn't strong enough to change the prejudice against them. Mom had worked as a clippie and had raised me. Even so, secretly, and sometimes openly, society had looked down upon her and she had suffered.
I suggested matrimony to Arthur many times, and he slipped like an eel. Eventually, I left him. When I heard that you were in

Living in the past (and present)

the family way, my heart bled for you. Your Dad was quite right to grab him by the neck and force him to marry you.

Thank you for inviting me for the service to see the face of a man who had just reached the end of the line!

Champika Wijayaweera

Nick

Charm: to bewitch, influence as if by magic, captivate and delight.

Some have a distinct lack of charm. It is a shame that the distribution of charm amongst the populace is not determined by the moral worth of the individual. For the moral can lack charm and the immoral possess it in abundance. Those who are charming may be unaware that they are so but, conversely, an individual may be perfectly aware that they are charming. It is the latter who, if also immoral, may well misuse their blessing.

There is Nick - in the wedding photograph two back from the groom. If it had not been for the medical exemption, why of course he would have been with Arthur doing his bit.

The photograph does not do him justice for, in the flesh, he was handsome indeed. And charming. And he knew it. His fellow men would marvel at his effect on the vast majority of females he encountered. His enemies, and there were some, would despair at how easily they succumbed. For the matter of attraction to the opposite sex is another of life's perplexities. For just as men will dismay at how easily so many females seem to be swayed by one of their own sex, a male so transparently what used to be termed a 'cad', then so too women will despair at how certain of their own sex, so transparently what used to be termed 'tarty', will charm and seduce even the most cerebral of males.

"Nick," Violet said, "you won't ruin my day will you?"
"What do you take me for Vi?"
"Sorry Nick, I do want you to come. As Arthur's best friend you have to come."
"Did you not want anyone at your wedding who has been more than a friend?"

Living in the past (and present)

"We both know that was a big mistake Nick. Arthur must never ever know. You promise me you will never tell him."
"Cross my heart and hope to die old girl."

Well, despite all the rubble and Violet's guilty secret, the wedding day went well. Afterwards Nick would visit the newlyweds and never mention what happened between him and Violet that time when Arthur was away fighting for his country. Well, loneliness and the war may have been an excuse. They were not the only ones acting out of character. Well, Violet anyway. Nick knew exactly what he was doing.

That is until one day when Nick called when Arthur was back overseas with the regiment.
"You had better not come in Nick, Arthur's away."
"If you want me to keep our little secret you are stuck with me, old girl. Now let me in and give me a proper welcome."

Richard Blakemore

The bridesmaid's story

I'm sorry to say this, but Vi made me really cross at first. The town centre bombed to smithereens, hundreds of people lying dead and all she could do was bawl her eyes out because the church she and Arthur were due to get married in on Monday had been destroyed. She was lying on her bed, the pink eiderdown all crumpled and damp from her tears, sobbing her heart out.

I said to her, 'Don't be so selfish Vi. Think of all those poor dead people and the ones who've lost their homes,' but she wouldn't have it. I tried another tack. 'Put if off. Marry Arthur on his next leave,' but she said they didn't know when that would be, and besides.

I said, 'Besides what,' and then I knew.

'Oh Vi, you're not.'

She started to cry again. 'Don't tell mum and dad; they'd kill me.'

'How far gone are you.'

'Not very.'

'You don't think you're just late?'

'No. I've been sick in the mornings and I can't stand the smell of the bread in the bakery.'

'Oh Blimey. That looks serious. I didn't even know you and Arthur had, well, you know, done it. I mean you haven't seen him for three months so that means, oh my God, you must be nearly four months gone. At least you're not showing yet but you won't have long.'

Vi gave me a look and then I knew something else. 'Oh don't tell me it isn't Arthur's.'

She started to cry again. 'It was after that raid in October. Remember that dance in the church hall when the siren went? I was with Nick and he told me he knew a place we'd be safe. But he didn't take me to a shelter, he took me onto the Common. I was ever so cold so he took off his jacket and put it round me and then one thing led to another.'

She started to cry again. 'We did it standing up. Dot at the bakery said if you did it standing up you wouldn't fall pregnant, but I know now that's not true.'

I sat on the bed and put my arm round her. 'Don't worry duckie. We'll speak to Canon Merry, tell him Arthur's only got a 48-hour pass and you don't know when you'll see him again. There's a war on; this kind of thing happens all the time. On your wedding night, pretend it hurts and Arthur'll never know.'

'I hate deceiving Arthur. I do love him you know.'

I had my doubts but said, 'I know you do, but what else do you think you can do? Tell him you're having another man's kiddie and expect him to be pleased about it? He'd throw you over Vi and then where would you be? And another thing, Nick must never know it's his kiddie either. He's a rum lot and I can see him using this to stir up a bit of trouble in the future. He'd enjoy that.'

'Oh God Betty, what a mess.'

'There aren't many messes that can't be sorted. You dry your eyes. I'll tell mum you're upset because you thought the wedding would be off and then we'll go and speak to Canon Merry.'

'Oh Betty, thanks for this, you are good.'

'Not that good lovie. It's the good ones that get caught.'

'What d'you mean Betty. Are you saying..?'

I put my finger to my lips. 'I won't tell mum about you and you won't tell her about me. All right?'

'All right. Oh I wish I could be like you Betty, you know so much stuff, you're so wise.'

'No you don't. You wouldn't like the way I had to find it all out. Now, come on, comb your hair and put on a bit of warpaint and we'll go downstairs.'

She gave me a sideways look and got up from the bed, absently running her hands over her stomach. Yes, we really needed to see Canon Merry and get the job done.

Years later, I wondered how I did that because, you see, it was *my* Arthur she was marrying. He'd gone out with me first. We'd started as friends but then I fell for him only he didn't look on me in the same way. He used to say, 'Betty, you're the best friend a bloke could ever have. In fact, I think of you as being a bloke. You can take that as a compliment.' I used to smile and laugh but how I wished it could have been more. And I wasn't at all flattered that he thought of me just as another bloke.

I don't know how I got through that wedding. I'm glad it was cold because that accounted for why I was shaking in my bridesmaid's dress. But I had to watch Vi marrying Arthur, *my* Arthur, all the time wishing it was me standing there next to him. It seemed right that the church was in ruins because the whole thing was a ruin as far as I was concerned. To make matters worse, Nick turned up for the wedding and I didn't want to have to speak to him.

But when we were at the Fox and Grapes after, for the reception, he came up to me in his smarmy way and said, 'Pleased to see your Vi getting married. Arthur's a lucky bloke.'

'He certainly is,' I said, without so much as a flicker.

'Listen,' he said, 'weddings always make me feel a bit romantic. Why don't you and I nip off somewhere else and get to know each other better.'

'You're right. They make me feel romantic too, so if you'll excuse me, I'll go and talk to Raymond,' and off I went without a backward look.

Judy Theobald

The bridegroom's story

Quassassin Camp, Egypt, June 1941.
Not long now until we go up the blue and quite frankly, I'll be relieved. I've just had letters from home - Vi's dad telling me to behave myself, like I'd have any option not to in this fly-blown dump, and one from Betty, telling me how fed up Vi is with being pregnant. Still nothing from Joaney.

It's so bloody hot here. Can't believe just over six months ago we were freezing our nuts off in that ruined church. I was so glad when it was bombed; I thought I'd get out of the wedding but Vi, Betty and their mum had other ideas. And to be perfectly frank, I certainly don't think her dad would have let me get out of it either. On my previous leave he'd come home early and caught us in their front room, me with my hand up her skirt thinking I might get a bit of how's-your-father.

He drags me out into the passage and pins me against the wall. 'That's it, you dirty little bugger. If you don't marry her now, I'll see you bloody live to regret it.' I'll be honest with you, I was scared. But I could see there were advantages. Her dad owned the garage I worked in. Betty, her sister, worked there too, not in the office but with us lads, as a mechanic. I always thought she was a bit unnatural myself, but she was a great laugh and we got on like a house on fire. Then I had to think about after the war, if I needed a job there'd be one at the garage, and looking even further into the future, there was also a business to inherit at some time.

But on top of it all, there was this other thing, I'd been going out with Joan who worked in the office – what a corker. Then she dumped me. I was pretty cut up and I suppose I'd only gone out with Vi on the rebound and to try to make Joan jealous. Anyway, I asked Vi to marry me. Fortunately, I had my dead mum's engagement ring, so I didn't have to lay out any cash. She seemed quite pleased with it and thank the lord it fitted so I didn't even have to get it altered.

When I got called up it seemed natural I should join the REME, 'rough engineering made easy', her dad called it but I didn't care. It got me out of that mess for a while. After I finished training, we'd have a few days' leave so Vi and her mum did all the arrangements for the wedding. I reckon Hitler did his best for me, bombing the church when he did, but thanks to Betty sticking her oar in, the whole thing went ahead in the ruins.

And what a ruin it was. After the ceremony, I couldn't believe it when I turned round and there's Joaney, standing there, smiling and laughing like she's just won the pools. At the reception she came up to me and said, 'Done well for yourself there, Arthur. Don't mess it up like you did with me.' Blimey, how did she find out about me and the barmaid at The Anchor? Women are so unforgiving – one little mistake and they never let you forget it.

So here I am, a respectable married man with a kiddie due in two months' time. Two months – who knows, I might be dead by then. Can't say it really bothers me. She'll be able to tell the nipper that his, or her, dad was a war hero. Yes I could live with that. Live with that? Do you hear me? The only way I can be a hero now is to die.

Judy Theobald

The wedding that should never have been

Another day imprisoned here in this photograph. The lights switch on at 10.00 a.m. and we are laid bare once more. Today a writing group gathers round, pens poised. "This is the one I'd like you to consider writing about," chirps up their leader. "Something fictional, factual or fantastical, your choice." They nod in agreement.

How I would like, just once, to be able to see how nearly they can really see into my life, my soul. Staring back at you dressed in my bridal gown I want to shout out loud, "You know nothing, nothing about me. You cannot possibly imagine the life that was mine on this day, December 2nd 1940."

They have stared at us, scribbled and moved on but you are still here looking intently into my eyes: "Can you see my anguish, my sorrow?"
"Yes, I see it; but this surely should have been one of the happiest days of your life. I am listening and hearing you so go on please."
"You see me as I stand between my future husband, Arthur, and my determined intransigent father. I approached this day with a very heavy heart. Arthur had loved me since our childhood days, the boy next door, the trusted friend, my father's choice. He fitted Dad's bill of dependable and reliable and he was fighting for our country...I fought them both off for months, dreaming up a million reasons why it wouldn't work for me. I can hear by your sighs that you are beginning to understand my reason.

Freddie, my dear beloved, had come into my life just before the war started and we knew within weeks that we wanted to spend our lives together. Then things happened very quickly when he had to go for basic training and from there to France. We barely had time for good-byes, just one stolen night together. Then nothing, just silence. Freddie never replied to my letters and news of his regiment was thin on the ground. By now the banns had been read in church and I began to regret that stolen night of love and doubt Freddie's true love for me.

So here I am in this photograph, browbeaten into submission and about to recite my vows."
"So that is why you look so unhappy."
"No, you don't understand, how could you? Look carefully towards the rear of this photograph: do you see the handsome man with a lock of black hair hanging over his eye? That's my beloved Freddie returned this very morning, my wedding day, but too late to save me."
"So here you stand frozen in time reliving this day over and over again: how tragic."
"Please allow us to rest in peace now, ask them to rip up this picture so that Freddie and I can join our hands together for eternity."

Val Claisse

Life in the Workhouse

While searching for resources relating to the locations of different trades and occupations in Southampton's varied neighbourhoods, we came across an archive recounting the story of the city's workhouse. Memories of grandparents' terror of 'ending up in the workhouse' surfaced - why was this such a terrible thing?

Serendipity plays a larger part in creativity than we might expect. Reading through the conditions that inmates endured, and listening to oral history recordings, triggered us to imagine what it must have been like ...

Hollybrook Children's Home 1941

Lockdown Virtual Tours of Southampton's Buildings, Monuments and Memorials.

Number 1: Workhouses.

"Right, now that we're all here, we can begin our Walking Tour of Southampton's Workhouses starting here outside God's House Tower. Unfortunately, the exact site of this city's first Workhouse is not known. It is recorded that in 1629 there was a £200 Bequest for a 'House of twelve rooms for the habitation of poor people'. In the next year the executor arranged with the Corporation, that on the building of the 'Poor House' the legacy should be devoted to the purchase of land for the poor to work on. Two years later premises were provided. The benefactor was a certain ... John Major ... certainly Southampton had a MP in 1628, so ... perhaps our ex Prime Minister will go on 'Who do you think you are' and they will trace his forebears right back to his MP namesake!

P. Mansell's 1771 Map shows a Workhouse by Winkle Street which may be the site of the first 'Poor House'. Please ask any questions at any point ... Wherever it was, records show that the original buildings by 1668 had fallen into a bad state and the Workhouse was transferred to French Street .... So follow me please, it's just a short walk across High Street and along Porters Lane. Please keep together and follow my Southampton FC umbrella.... Here we are at the site of St John's Hospital founded in 1671 for 'the instruction of lads in the woollen trade'. The buildings later became a Georgian theatre and is now the block of flats that you see before you.

Follow me now please... Each parish was responsible for its own poor, so we are now crossing into Bugle Street which was then in a different parish. It was here that in 1753, under the provisions of Knatchbull's Act of 1723, that five parishes set up a Common Workhouse at Bugle Hall here at the south west junction of Bugle Street and West Gate. Previous owners of the

Hall included Henry Wriothesley, Earl of Southampton - and Shakespeare's patron. It was destroyed by fire in 1791 ... Now it is here in Cuckoo Lane that we can still see the two pillars that originally formed a gateway to the garden.

We now need to take a little walk to the junction of St Mary's Place and Chapel Street because in 1773 Southampton's Poor Law Incorporation was formed. It decided to sell the old St John's site and the £425 was then used to build a new Workhouse on the north side of St Mary's Church.

However, as its capacity was only 220 inmates, it could only accommodate about a fifth of the city's paupers. By 1843 the residents were four to a bed with no segregation of the sexes and increasingly insanitary conditions. In 1865 a Poor Law Inspector roundly condemned the 'mixing together of all classes, including the old, the infirm and the idiots in rooms in which it is almost impossible for human beings to live'.

It was then decided to build a new Workhouse on land adjoining the existing site. The front contained the Master's quarters and accommodation for the able bodied, then the aged, the Infirmary block and the Infectious Wards. Across the road were the Boys' and Girls' Schools in two converted houses.
It wasn't until 1904 that, to protect them from disadvantage in later life, the birth certificates of those born in the Workhouse gave its address as '154 St Mary Street' which is where you stand now.

In 1940 it became an Emergency Food Centre and housed homeless families. Work began in 1947, to convert it to a Technical College. In 1995 it became Southampton City College.

Living in the past (and present)

That ends our Hidden History's Walk around Southampton's Workhouses. I hope that this will prove useful to you all with your writing.

Peter Nicol-Harper

My early life

You may be surprised that I count myself one of the lucky ones, when you read that I lived ten years of my life in an 'institution.'

Mum was 20 and unmarried when she had me. Her Dad called her a dirty whore and kicked her out. Her sister put her up for a while but when she did it again, when I was three, she couldn't afford to keep us all now that I had a baby brother. I don't remember any of what went on except that Mum cried a lot and I was always cold and hungry.

We had nowhere to live, so ended up in a workhouse, which was a deeply shameful place to be. The place smelled of carbolic and boiled cabbages but it was warm and nobody shouted. Mum looked sad all the time and there were a lot of old ladies scrubbing wooden floors, always in complete silence. The food was the same each day: soup, meat and veg: nothing fancy but my tummy felt full.

After a few months we were up and off again. I remember Mum sitting me down and telling me that I was her best girl and she wanted me to show the nice people there what a good girl I was. Then she gave me a big kiss and held my head in her hands and looked at me for a long time and then she was gone.

I lived at Oaklands children's home until I was 8. I made a few friends and we had food every day. We all had our jobs to do, everything followed a routine. Each morning we were marched in a crocodile to Hollybrook school. I loved it there: the teachers' smiled and sometimes patted my shoulder which made me feel good. No one touched us at the Home. When I was 8 I went to a smaller home nearby, Hollybrook. Here they taught us how to cook simple meals and clean a house but none of the grown-ups ever really had a proper conversation with us.

Living in the past (and present)

One day, when I was 12, a new boy arrived, up from Oaklands. The matron called me to her room, 'Mary, this is your brother Robert, I don't know why no-one told you before, you can show him round the Home before teatime'. I was completely shocked. Robert had sat next to me at mealtimes for four years at Oaklands and not one of the adults had seen fit to tell me.

I remember feeling a combination of deep anger and sorrow. Here was someone I could have loved and cared for. It still pains me now to think of all those lost years. I had not seen my mother since I was four: the Homes didn't encourage visits, apparently. She turned up to collect me when I was twelve. Poor Robert was left behind because he was too young to go to work. That was a very sad parting for us, but when you have been institutionalised you learn to bottle things up and move on.

I know now that school was my salvation. Being able to read and write opened up lots of opportunities. So, I didn't have to wash sheets in the laundry. I got a job in the corner shop and was soon trusted enough to take money.

When we were in the Home Mum's sister said she could stay with her. Mum was then able to earn enough to pay towards our 'keep'. So, in an odd sort of way being in the workhouse and the Home saved me from the poverty of the streets and gave me an education.

I don't feel bitter about my childhood, but it has taken a good many years for me to learn to be loving and to love.

Val Claisse

Hollybrook girl

VE day 1995 - Elsie responds to her granddaughters' questions about her life in the war:

It was the war that gave me an escape, you see. I mean, domestic service wasn't that bad, and you got your afternoon off every week, but it was long hours, and all 'Yes ma'am, no ma'am, three bags full ma'am' – nearly as bad as the workhouse itself. Speaking up wasn't encouraged there, either. You didn't have that much choice when you left the children's home - you had to have work where you lived in, otherwise you'd spend most of your wages on rent. And landlords were chary of single girls - thought you were on the game.

I never knew my Ma – she died when I was a few hours old, so I grew up in the Hollybrook children's homes. They were called 'cottages', but where I lived was quite a substantial house in Seymour Road. There was a housemother: she had her favourites, who somehow got to stay up later and listen to the wireless. I wasn't one of those. It's not that I was rude or anything, but I never had the kind of cute smile that made grown-ups want to do something special for you.

I did alright at school – I wasn't dim and I liked reading. Being dim was dreadful: 'imbeciles' they used to call them, you know: the dotty old ladies who'd been through too much and lived in their own daydreaming worlds. I didn't like having to take the laundry up to those wards. Or 'feebleminded' – I'm sure my Ma can't have been one of those, because I passed some exams to get into the Wrens. Heredity's a funny thing: your Mum joined that family history group, and tried to find out more about my Ma and where she came from... I don't think she got very far ...

I remember the coronation of the old king – it was my last week in the cottage before I entered service – a photographer turned up to take a picture of us all. Those hideous uniforms we had to wear. I was determined that when I started earning, I'd get pretty clothes. My first year of work, I saved up my wages to buy fabric to make some nice things, and that was what I spent my money on for the whole year. Well, I didn't have any family to go and visit, or buy birthday presents for, so I didn't need much.

Hours I spent in Plummers, looking at the clothes, seeing how they were put together. Dress patterns have always been pricey, so you learned to copy the pieces on tracing paper, and then alter them according to the style you wanted. My employer let us look at her magazines when she'd read them, so after Cook and the parlourmaid had finished, I got them to keep.

Going to the pictures on my afternoon off was mainly where I decided which fashions I liked. Carole Lombard was my favourite: she had so much energy, and Merle Oberon was really glamorous. Sometimes I bumped into other girls from school, but mostly they pretended not to know me.

I'd learned to sew at school – girls did, back then – and by the time I left to join the Wrens, I had clothes that looked nice – that fitted properly, and showed my figure. Not that I got to wear them much, though at least the Wren uniform was smart. Some of the other girls moaned about the discipline – it felt quite a doddle to me after school holidays slaving in the workhouse laundry!

I don't know why I applied to become a mechanic – had enough of laundry and scrubbing, and I wasn't the right class to work in an office. Best decision of my life – not just because that's where I met your Grandad, God bless him. We got to travel, you see – anywhere the ships went, we were at the base to carry out repairs. It was hard work, but satisfying, and I would

Living in the past (and present)

have carried on if I hadn't got married. But when your Grandad proposed, well, that meant the chance to have a home of my own. I don't know why you girls are so snooty about being 'just a housewife', because, for me, that was all I'd ever wanted.

Susy Churchill

Neighbourhoods

Back in the nineteenth century, when Southampton enjoyed a brief spell of popularity as a spa town, wealthy merchants built country houses in extensive grounds in the south Hampshire countryside. Changes in fortune and fashion mean that few of these survive.

In his 1931 book, 'Southampton: A Civic Survey', Ford wrote "the paradox of Southampton: It is not the countryside which has created Southampton: Southampton is recreating the countryside." The docks were the reason for the existence of our city, but people who live and work in the docks need local farms to provide their food, brewers to produce their ale, tailors and builders and ironmongers to house and clothe them ...

Census data show that incomes have always been lowest in the St Mary's and 'Town' areas. The streets surrounding the Common have been the most affluent neighbourhoods since the start of the twentieth century. We explored a range of archives, and drew on family memories, to create the following pieces.

Living in the past (and present)

Bitterne Manor House

All of this is absolutely true (except for a few embellishments.)

Hello. My name is Mr Field. Actually, it's double-barrelled, but I don't always use all of it.

You know all about how many owners of ancestral homes boast that their great-great to the power-of-whatever grandfather has continuously occupied their 'pile' going as far back as, say, the Normans. Well, you may be surprised to hear that my family tree shows that we have continuously occupied Bitterne Manor land for at least two thousand years.

My forebears were living here when the Romans arrived in what they named Clausentum. The reason I know this is because although my distant relations obviously didn't record anything in writing, my research into Roman writing tablets has made a gruesome discovery. The Romans practiced cannibalism! I can imagine that my ancestors were initially prepared to live peacefully alongside the invaders. But as soon as they had killed and eaten one of us I know that my descendants must have gone into hiding.

Four hundred years later the Romans departed and my past generations were still there when the stones from the Roman buildings were used to build the original Manor House in Norman times.
And they are mentioned as still living there when the Bishop of Winchester's Travelling Court used the River Itchen to visit. The Manor Farm House was then being used as a distribution centre for wine and salt panned from the tidal river.

Living in the past (and present)

In 1274 Robert Kilwardby, the then Archbishop of Canterbury, is recorded as staying over Christmas when my family were there. Scarcity of labourers for Manor House Farm resulting from the Black Death of 1348 led to higher running costs and so it became more profitable to let part of the house to tenants for almost the next 500 years.
In 1804-5 the Farmhouse was demolished and a new Manor House constructed. Although it was not easy, my distant relations managed to stay on site throughout.

During WW2 bombing raids severely damaged our House and made it almost uninhabitable. Although we continued to live there we couldn't prevent parts of it later being vandalised. Fortunately, a local architect Herbert Collins converted it into 14 flats and on the 14th of July 1953 it became Grade 2 listed.

And now we finally reach the present day, so let me introduce you to my family. In Flat Number 1 with me is my partner Minnie. Next door has become a Granny Flat where her father Marcus is looking after his parents. In other flats my sisters Felicity and Amelia are bringing up my twin nephews Ferdinand and Mortimer. We are all very happy here and would love to stay here for generations to come.

Unfortunately, some other residents seem to be complaining about "Infestation" and want us to be "exterminated". They are committing 'Hate Crime'. They are now calling us "vermin", so who knows what the future holds? After over 2000 years of continuous occupation will the proud Mouse family of Bitterne Manor cease to be allowed to continue to live here?

Peter Nicol-Harper

Freemantle in 1908

We were lucky really – after they'd pulled down Freemantle House they sold off the land and built our streets. They were nice houses, and near enough to the docks so Jim could get to the ships easily. Everyone round here had family members at sea – it held us all together. Lots of wives lost their husbands through hard work or accidents or just falling overboard, so you needed to keep in with your neighbours. Some of the trees from the house's grounds were still standing and there was a lake, though we didn't really like the small children to go there on their own. I liked it because I'd been brought up in the countryside. My father worked on a farm but there wasn't so much work like that around and lots of people moved into town. But it was good, we had everything we needed here, including a corner shop where they even kept a cow out the back so we always had fresh milk.

Jim was a fireman though in the end he became a ship's engineering labourer which wasn't that much better. It was a tough job, working below sea level, shovelling coal to keep the boilers running. Ships don't stop at night so they had to work four hours on, four hours off, 24 hours a day. When they weren't working they slept in a dormitory, a couple of dozen men all sharing the same sleeping space. Sometimes he was away for months on end but when he came home he made up for it; we had eleven children and I'm pleased to say, we only lost the one.

I've heard miners' wives like to say they had it tough but at least their men came home every night and shared their bed. We were left alone for weeks or months on end, managing the house and the children and when our men came home – if they came home, for many were lost at sea – they were exhausted. My Jim died at 46; his poor heart gave out, and I was left with the youngest children to bring up on my own. I took in washing and my older sons Jim and Fred were still with me; they worked as boilermakers so they helped with the money. The older ones had already gone; Rosina did a flit and married but has had so many children I doubt she'll last long. Jack had got himself a very comfortable apprenticeship at a boot and shoemaker. Ellen was in service and doing very nicely. Her employer, Mr Williams, lived with his sister. She'd been engaged to a doctor but when he found out their mother was in an asylum, he called it off. That's why neither of them ever married, in case the madness was passed on to another generation, but at least it meant there wouldn't be any children for Ellen to look after.

She was a parlour maid, no rough work, and they treated her very well. She had her own bed and she only had to share the room with one other maid, Rose. On one of her days off she met a young lad on the Common and they started walking out. I wasn't too sure about him at first as he'd never had a proper job but then Mr Williams pulled a few strings and got him into the Southampton police force so Ellen will be set up for life. Mr Williams let her use the big dining room table to cut out and make her wedding dress – in fact, she made her whole trousseau there. They made a handsome couple at their wedding and I couldn't be more pleased.

Henry is still with me but not for much longer. He's been working as an errand boy but soon he'll be going to sea and working, like his father on the ships, starting out as a trimmer. His job will be to shovel the coal in such a way the ship isn't unbalanced, stays in trim. Hard work and I don't want to see him go but there's not much more people from round here can do. I expect the other girls will go into service and I hope my William won't have to go to sea. Just as it was with Jim, every time he'll go off, I'll wonder if I'll ever see him again.

Judy Theobald

North Stoneham House and the Willis-Fleming family

This lost country house in Hampshire formed part of the Willis-Fleming estate which existed for at least 350 years from 1599 to the 1950s. In the 17th and early 18th centuries the 400-acre North Stoneham estate was owned by the Fleming family. In 1737 it passed to their distant relatives the Willis family who added the Fleming surname to their own. In 1778 the estate was improved by the famous landscape gardener Capability Brown. The old manor house was pulled down in 1818 and construction was started on a larger Greek Revival style mansion which took about 25 years and cost about £100,000. This was titled North Stoneham House.

In the 19th century John Barton Willis-Fleming was one of the largest landed proprietors in Hampshire, the Fleming estate extending to 15,000 acres. The estate centred on North Stoneham Park with property in Eastleigh, Swaythling, South Stoneham, Bassett, Chilworth, North Baddesley, Chandlers Ford and Romsey, and also on the Isle of Wight at Binstead and Arreton among others.

There were some fine country houses on these lands, including Chilworth Manor, a much smaller house, which still exists today as a hotel. The grandiose North Stoneham house was never completed or fully occupied. In 1860 the family moved to Chilworth Manor. Stoneham then became home to several families between the 1860s and 1930s, all living in different parts of the house.

In 1914 the British government offered Belgian refugees hospitality, beginning the largest refugee movement in British history. At North Stoneham Commandant le Chevalier Georges de Melotte, and his wife Marie Louise and their children, stayed as guests of the Willis-Fleming family for a year. Later the disused part of North Stoneham park was converted into a hospital for wounded Belgians, with beds for 50 soldiers. The mansion's spectacular circular hall became the hospital's "smoking room," with the flags of Great Britain, its allies, and the Red Cross suspended from the gallery. The Eastleigh Locomotive works raised money for the hospital, and local allotment holders donated vegetables. The house was finally demolished in 1939. The stable block remains as a guest house at Park Farm as does a beautiful war shrine in the park grounds. During the Great War there was a popular movement for making wayside shrines.

The shrine was built in 1917 by John Willis-Fleming as a war memorial to his son Richard and the other thirty six men of North Stoneham parish who died in the Great war. In recent years this shrine has been sensitively restored by Eastleigh Borough council and the Willis-Fleming Historical Trust.

John's son Richard was killed in action at the battle of Romani, Egypt on the 4th August 1916, the day after his 20th birthday. His commanding officer made a drawing of Richard's temporary grave and wrote. "An English Gentleman is what I would call

Living in the past (and present)

him, although not a typical one, as that would not be a very praiseworthy attribute, but an Ideal English Gentleman - an ideal man." Richard is buried at Kantara War Memorial Cemetery in Egypt. Like all British soldiers in the Great War, his body was never returned home.

Richard kept a daily diary whilst he served overseas which makes very interesting reading.

Val Claisse

References: The Willis-Fleming Historic Trust papers.

Summer holidays

Miss Sherwood stood at the gate in her white cotton coat and black beret, holding her lolly-pop stick and waiting for the first of the children to run out. The bell rang and she smiled to think of what would happen in the next few minutes – as it did every year as the summer term ended. The doors opened and the children emerged – first a trickle and then more and more as the excitement became contagious.

Peter started the chant and Kevin and Brian joined in, followed by Terry and Chris. Then Carol and Brenda and lots of other girls took it up, over and over again they all chanted. The noise became louder and louder and soon the younger children took it up.
"No more days of school, no more days of sorrow, no more days of this old dump, we're staying home tomorrow".

"Bye, Miss Sherwood. Bye, hope you and Scotty have a good holiday," said Carol as she jumped onto the number 79A bus, swirled around the post on the platform and waved.

Jumping off the bus just as it stopped, Pete and Carol raced each other home and their mum was waiting indoors with jam sandwiches, orange squash and a big smile.
"Off you go then. Get changed and out to play. You've got an hour and then Auntie Marge and I have a surprise for you."

Carol changed into her old playing-out clothes and plimsolls and ran over to Brenda's house to knock on the door.
"Coming out, Bren'? Let's have a game of hop-scotch. We'll go and get Jean and Sandra and mark it out on the pavement. I've got some chalk and you can find some good pebbles to throw."
"Do you think Beryl Hall will want to play too?" said Brenda, looking worried.

"Don't worry about her, Bren'. If she comes out I'll just tell her she can join in but only if she's nice to you and if she isn't then we'll just cut her out and not talk to her. Anyway, you know that she won't ever win, she's so clumsy and can't jump further than number 4, so she'll make some excuse and go away."

The girls started to play. They were all so excited that the summer holidays had started. After hop-scotch they played Queenie, Queenie, Who's Got The Ball with lots of the other girls on the estate. Some of the younger ones joined in as well but they weren't very good at catching. Later on the girls got together with Pete and some of the other boys and prepared for a quick game of Kick the Can. Carol collected a few pieces of dried grass and held them out and the one who drew the shortest piece of grass had to go first to count to 100 while the others ran and hid. The first to get back and kick the can before the counter tagged them was the winner. It was a good game but Pete and Carol only had time for one round before their mum called them indoors.

Carol and Pete were excited to see what the surprise was and they saw there was a picnic ready in Mum's cloth bags, with 3 bottles of pop and lots of sandwiches packed in greaseproof paper. There were also pieces of pork pie and hard-boiled eggs. Auntie Marge's boys, Brian and Chris' and their little sisters, Kathy and Claire were also waiting and then they all set off. They walked all the way through the woods to the shore and then along the gravel path to Warsash Point, which was one of their favourite places. They were allowed to paddle in the river and Mum and Auntie Marge joined in too and they were all laughing and splashing each other.

Just as they were getting dried off Pete spotted the Queen Mary coming down Southampton Water and they watched her make her way into the Solent, as they ate their picnic. She was enormous and Mum said only rich people could go on her and that she was going all the way across the Atlantic Ocean to New York, in America.

After a good game of hide and seek they all began their slow walk home and Pete and Brian carried the little girls on their backs for part of the way because they were so tired.

Pete said that tomorrow he and Brian, Chris and Kevin were going down the woods to see what they could find and that they would call in and see if John could come out with them. John lived in a big house down in Holly Hill Lane. His mum made really tasty, thick biscuits called Parkin and John had two great, friendly dogs, called George and Ben. Pete loved running with George and Ben. He wished he could have a dog of his own. Carol said that tomorrow she and her friends would play skipping with the long rope and see who could do the bumps and jump in the fastest. Carol loved the songs they chanted when they played:

'Janey and Johnny
Sitting in a tree,
K-I-S-S-I-N-G
First comes love,
Then comes marriage
Then comes Janey
With a baby carriage.'

Also:
'I like coffee,
I like tea,
I'd like for Jenny
To jump in with me.'

School summer holidays were so much fun.

Lindsey Neve

58

Tudor House: the great survivor

As it was first built in the 1180s this house should perhaps then have been referred to as "Norman" House. It coped with the French Raid in 1338 and the Black Death in 1347.

When it was over 350 years old it could truly first become known as Tudor House when its owner provided lodgings for privateers and sailors. It now contains one of the finest examples of Tudor graffiti.

By the late 19th century it had become part of Southampton's worst slums with limited running water and malnourished, disease-ridden tenants. In 1886 it was threatened with demolition.

It survived the First World War and the Spanish Flu pandemic. In 1940 the Museum's curator Edward Judd used the wine cellar as an Air Raid Shelter during the Southampton Blitz when a house two doors down was destroyed.

At the end of the 20th century it was fairly dilapidated due to a combination of poor renovation and the passage of over 800 years. A 1999 Survey stated that the house was "opening like the petals of a flower" that is, bowing outwards.

As well as the aforementioned problems that Tudor House has outlived, can be added leprosy, yellow fever, cholera, smallpox, tuberculosis, typhus fever, measles, swine flu, zika and ebola, so I am confident that, post-coronavirus, it is only a matter of time until the Tudor House Museum re-opens and thrives again.

Peter Nicol-Harper

A personal snapshot of Southampton and environs

Down at heel Shirley
Discounts and charities
A street without style.
Tired and worried people
Making ends meet.

Students populate Portswood
The fashion-conscious young,
Coffee shops and yummy mums
Middle class schooling
For aspirational Uni-folk.

Bitterne, a windy outpost
For forgotten people on
the wrong side of the tracks.
A place without heart.

Woolston slowly closing down,
Whilst awaiting resurrection
from promised developments.
Too late to save old traders.

High street city centre
The council tries too hard,
Keeps moving the heart and the goalposts.
Bland, modern, urban, soulless,
With some nods to culture and history.

Netley Abbey
Charming Victorian outpost,
Attracting tourists to parks and beaches
And HOME for me!

Val Claisse

Southampton in World War 2

By the end of the 1930s, Southampton was an international seaport with an aircraft factory, as well as other key industries, so its destruction was part of the Germans' strategy to conquer Britain. But despite the Luftwaffe having such specific targets, many residential areas were also bombed. One thousand buildings were completely destroyed and just shy of 44,000 were damaged. Knowing their vulnerability, from the outset of the war people took action to protect themselves. On 1 and 2 September, 1939, the town's children were evacuated to south coast seaside resorts and many of the people who remained behind, built air-raid shelters in their gardens.

Changes Don't Happen; They Are Made

Last night, dressed in fancy clothes,
with happy buddies, his grandson
boarded a plane to the continent
to watch Harry Kane kicking goals.

Many years ago, his big brother,
with uniformed others, left home
to fly Spitfires to the continent:
perilous solo rides on tracer-lit sky

Care to bet a tenner for the winner,
grandson texted, Singing, dancing and booze
here, the vibes are awesome!
We are painting the town red (and white)

Inside the Bible mother read every night
he found the last letter from her firstborn:
The atmosphere is pretty grim here, but
we will give all for peace for all.

Champika Wijayaweera

War and Peace and Hate and Love

"Gunther, Ich mochte, dass Siediese Studenten zu einem
Astaush mit Southampton England mitnehmen"
(Gunther, I want you to take some students on an exchange to
Southampton, England)
"Nein Herr Director, you know that I hate the English."

Gunther's grandfather hadn't survived being shot down over
Hampshire in his Focke-Wulf bomber during WW2. Growing
up Gunter had come to despise the occupying English armed
forces strutting around his home town of Monchengladbach
being rude and condescending to the locals.

Three weeks later in October Gunther found himself at
Chamberlayne School. One of his fellow teachers had cried off
sick and Gunther's tutor group had begged him not to allow the
trip to be cancelled.

As the days went by Gunther surprised himself by becoming
fond of the English students and their teachers. He got on
particularly well with the art teacher, Penny Davies. Gunther
told her that his mother was an oil painter and had introduced
Gunther to many famous painters, but that his favourites were
the Slade School of Art painters. He had always particularly
liked Paul Nash's work.

At the end of the Exchange, Gunther was delighted when Penny
invited him and his family to come and stay with them at the
beginning of the Xmas holidays. Gunther, of course, had
diplomatically never mentioned to Penny about his grandfather
and why Gunther had nearly not come on the Exchange.

So it was that in mid-December the Davies family told Gunther,
his wife and 13-year-old daughter that they had a surprise for
them. They were taken to Southampton Art Gallery and shown

Paul Nash's "Totes Meer" (Dead Sea) painting. Penny was expecting Gunther to be overjoyed to see a Nash original, but it showed the wreckage of German WW2 planes in a scrapyard in Cowley, Oxford. Gunther couldn't help but think of his grandfather and he became overwhelmed. Not wanting anyone to see how upset he was, he pretended that he suddenly badly needed the lavatory and quickly exited down the stairs.

At the bottom he turned left into an alcove which he expected would lead to the toilets. Glancing up he was stopped in his tracks by the lettering.
"The SIRENS sounded.
It looked exactly like a ladder falling from the plane.
We felt a tremendous
SHUDDERING
Of the building
That quick memory has stayed with me in all its VIVIDNESS
I lost some of my classmates
It was a TERRIBLE day for us all"

The plaque confirmed Gunther's worst fears. On November 6th 1940 a 500 lb incendiary bomb hit the Civic Centre Art School killing 17 children.

Fortunately for Gunther, it was at this moment that Penny finally found him. Gunther gabbled to her that he couldn't stop himself from thinking that it might have been his grandfather that had dropped that bomb.

Penny told him that following that bombing and a subsequent weekend Blitz the decision was taken for a second evacuation of women and children from Southampton. And that surely must have saved the lives of many more children. In addition, she told him that Southampton Council subsequently resolved to prioritise funding to the Art Gallery.

Living in the past (and present)

They committed themselves to the principle that "the use of Art to stimulate and educate both young and adult minds alike is vital to the growth of the community". It was with that thought in his mind that Gunther was able to return to the Gallery and see indeed that Southampton now has one of the best art galleries in Britain.

Blitz memorial Southampton Central Library

Peter Nicol-Harper

Air raid

By the time Bert and Nellie got down to the kitchen, Bill was already standing by the back door, wagging his tail, ready to be let out. He was always first when the siren sounded. Bob joined them. 'I can't believe it mother. It's two o'ruddy clock. They've left it late tonight. I thought the blighters were going to let us off.'

'Language please Bob.' Nellie turned out the light, opened the door and watched Bill scamper down the garden towards the shelter, his white body bobbing up and down in the dark night. She closed the door again, drew across the curtain, turned the light back on, and started gathering the items she always kept ready. Their routine was always the same.

First there was a vacuum flask of tea, along with a tin of biscuits which she handed to Bert.

Bob was collecting Bill's blanket from the conservatory while she checked the contents of an attache case; birth and marriage certificates, insurance documents, ration books, she counted them, yes, four still there, likewise their identity cards, then the deeds to the house, their wills, the Post Office savings book, Bob's asthma medicine, some aspirin and finally a packet of mints.

The last wail of the siren died down, replaced by the crump, crump, crump of the first distant bombs. Bert turned out the light and felt his way towards the back door.

'Hurry up Nellie. Come on. They're on their way.'

'They won't be here yet. You take the case and I'll see if Jane's coming.

But when she called through to her daughter, she was met with the usual refusal. 'I'm too tired mother. You go without me. If Hitler wants me, he can have me.' It was always the same.

Nellie tutted but set off down the garden, her path lit by the same full moon which guided the bombers. She made her way down the steps into the shelter, closed the door behind her and pulled across the curtain. Bob, settling himself in one of the top bunks, turned on the torch. Using its faint beam, Albert lit a candle and placed an earthenware flowerpot on top, hoping to generate a little warmth. Bill turned around three times then dropped onto his mat, his head between his front paws. She picked up his blanket and covered him, tucking the edges round his little body – it might be April but the shelter was cold. Finally, she took off her raincoat, spread it over her own bunk then slithered between icy sheets. Their routine was always the same.

Crump-crump, crump, came the bombs, a little closer now.
'Did you leave the back door unlocked Nellie?'
'Yes.'
'Good. Are you warm enough?'
'No.'
'You soon will be duckie.'
'I know.'
She wouldn't though. She lay there, conscious of wet earth less than an inch away on the other side of the shelter's metal wall. She tried to move her leg but the rest of the bunk felt cold and damp compared with the patch she had already slightly warmed. She heard snoring – Bob or Bill; it didn't matter, both seemed oblivious to the bombing. Albert lay opposite her, still and settled.

Crump, crump, crump-crump, then the roar of aircraft engines – a little closer now.
She had to think of a way of keeping warm. She didn't want to unmake their beds and bring them to the shelter each time, not with everything else they had to carry. Then she remembered some threadbare blankets she'd held onto. Useless on their own, they could be sandwiched together to make a single warm cover. Perhaps if she didn't put up the summer curtains this year, she'd stitch them round the blankets to make a kind of

quilt, just for the air raids. She'd do that tomorrow. The machine was still out from where she'd been putting the sheets sides to middle.

A massive explosion shook the shelter; silt rained down on them. Bob woke with a 'What the...?'. Albert sat up.
'That was close. Check the house father.'
'It wasn't that close. Some other poor devil's caught it.'
'Check the house, now. Jane's in there.'
Bob turned on the torch and Albert's pyjamaed legs swung over the edge of his bunk. Nellie made out his shape in the faint light as he shuffled towards the door.
'Torch out Bob.'
Darkness, then a faint grey light as Albert opened the door and felt his way up the steps, peered up the garden and returned.
'House still standing Nellie, and Mrs Dunmore's and the Baldocks. Nothing to worry about.'
'Still, it was close Bert.'
'Go back to sleep love. Jerry's had his go for tonight. He won't be back here.'
'Oh, and I suppose Hitler told you that.'
Bert sighed. She could hear his bedclothes flapping in the dark, the bunk creaking and then stillness. Despite Bert's confidence, from nowhere a roaring squadron of aircraft passed over their heads. She tensed, waiting for the whine then the explosion, terrified in case these were her last moments; delighted to have proved Bert wrong. The sound died away; Ashfield Road was clearly not one of the Luftwaffe's targets tonight.

The cold still gnawed into her. She thought of her son-in-law fighting in the desert but he wouldn't be warm either. In one of his rare letters home he'd told them how the day's scorching heat was always replaced with night-time frosts. Who'd have thought they'd have frosts in the desert. Jane had knitted him a scarf and gloves but he'd lost them when his tank had taken a direct hit and in what little free time she had she was now knitting him more.

Had she done right to store the bottled fruit in the spare bedroom? But then Edie had kept hers downstairs in the scullery and lost the lot when the landmine exploded six doors down. What a night that was – the poor Robinsons killed outright by blast; not a mark on them, and Edie cleaning up broken glass and sticky plum juice for weeks afterwards. Every time she thought she'd seen the last of it, she'd find another splinter in her slipper, or even worse, in someone's bare foot. Nellie thought of moving the fruit to the shelter but it wasn't as secure as the house; anyone could break in and steal it.

Perhaps the all-clear would sound soon but then she heard another wave of bombers, probably droning up Southampton Water. The docks were really getting it tonight.

Good job they had that rabbit. Bob said someone had brought half a dozen into his office at the Ordnance Survey. Imagine that – why would you take dead rabbits into the Ordnance Survey? Anyway, he'd brought one home and he and Bert had done the business with it. Two good meals they'd get off it. She'd have to make sure Bert didn't eat more than his fair share; she hadn't forgotten the herring incident when Jane was on the way. Him coming home from night duty like that and eating the one she was saving for her breakfast. She was so upset, the poor baby was born with a herring-shaped birthmark on her leg and Nellie had never quite forgiven him.

Despite the cold, she must have slept because she was woken by the all-clear. It was still dark and none of them moved so she drifted back into sleep. She was woken again by noises from the garage. For a brief moment she thought Nazi paratroopers may have landed and gone looking for petrol but when she looked at the time it was seven o'clock.

She quickly got up, put on her raincoat over her nightdress and left the shelter.

'Is that you Jane?'

'Yes mother. I'm off to work; just getting my bike.'

'Mind Bob's car.'

'Yes, I'm minding Bob's car.' Bob's car which hadn't been driven since 1941 thanks to petrol rationing.

'Have you had something to eat? Is the gas still on?'

'Yes. I've boiled the kettle and left some hot water for you.'

'Mind how you go dear. There was a heavy raid last night. Watch out for craters.'

'Yes mother. I'll remember to cycle round them. Thank you for warning me.'

She was so rude nowadays. Before the war she'd been so polite and well-mannered, especially when she sold hats to titled ladies in that posh shop. Then she found a job in the factory and when they wanted to promote her they were worried a woman wouldn't cope with the men's bad language. Cope? She seemed to be joining in. Nellie even heard her say 'damn' when she laddered her stocking last week and she certainly wouldn't have said that in peacetime.

By the time she'd seen Jane off, Bert and Bob were making their way down the garden, Bill at their heels.

'All's well Bert. Jane's gone to work. The gas is still on.'

In the kitchen she lit the stove. They hadn't drunk the flask of tea and she poured it into a saucepan to heat through – no point in wasting it. Bob and Bert went upstairs to get dressed while she went to the larder to get the breakfast things – porridge again, that and a bit of toast would stand by them until lunchtime. Then they could have that rabbit with a few spuds and carrots and she'd do a rice pudding in the oven at the same time to save gas. The end of the loaf could go in there as well, to dry out for breadcrumbs.

Living in the past (and present)

After breakfast, Bert would go out and inspect the local bomb damage like he always did, then later he'd plant out the onion sets. Once she'd cleared up the breakfast things and finished the housework, she'd make up those quilts for the shelter.
The sun was coming out, Bill snuffled around her feet, searching out interesting smells, Jane had already started work and Bob would be heading off soon. The conservatory windows had made it through the night so her tomato plants had survived unscathed. They were all still alive; it was a good day.

Judy Theobald

Sirens

Woolston, 30 November 1940

Esther shuddered as the air raid siren blared out: another night of fear and shivering. She grabbed her gas mask, handbag, umbrella, keys; pulled on her overcoat, and hurried out. Some of her colleagues went up to the Common, but she preferred to head for the shelter. She'd got into the habit of making sandwiches as soon as she got home from the factory, to take out with her, but tonight she'd managed to swallow her tea. Not that she had much of an appetite these days, but you had to carry on. Her landlord would be busy again tonight: so brave, doing fire watch. He looked so tired coming home at dawn, when the bombs finally stopped.

Some nights were easier, but they were relentless, the Luftwaffe – marauding bullies, following the example of the biggest bully. Other times were truly terrible: that wicked day, back in September, when planes had dived down, hidden by the sun, before the siren could sound. She'd been at work that day, but she heard about it.

There was another raid in October when a plane dived out of the clouds, with no sound until it started machine gunning people in the streets. They claimed to be Christians, but how many churches had the Luftwaffe destroyed? Nazi scum!

'Scum': how fluent she had become! Her old English teacher had said that fluency was being able to curse in another language. She had thought herself a good linguist, back in high school days, but school English had proved to be different from how people actually spoke. 'Actually' – another of those very English words she had struggled to master.

Living in the past (and present)

The sky was alight: incendiaries gave the air a lurid glow, combining with the smoke to make a scene from Hell. How much more could the city take? Would there be anything left? But it wasn't only the buildings that had been obliterated...they had all taken such a pounding this year, and people's tempers were fraying, worn out by nights of disturbed sleep.

You're still alive, Esther! And although working in a factory isn't what you imagined, this war must end one day. At least you got out in time – Liliane, Eva and the children must be dead by now. Why hadn't they listened to your warnings? She left when the first Aryanizations happened, five years ago now, but Eva's husband had just been appointed to a position at the Conservatoire, and Aunty Liane loved looking after the children while Eva worked at the kindergarten. They thought they'd be safe – Hitler loves music, after all.

Esther treasured a publicity photograph that showed them in their smart frocks, in the showroom. Viscose, of course, not real silk, so they could be laundered, but still soft to wear, and beautifully made. People were impressed when you said that you worked at Leopold Seligman's: one of Berlin's most prestigious fashion manufacturers. They looked so glamorous: Mr Seligman said they were like the Sirens who tried to lure Ulysses onto the rocks. Esther looked twenty years older now – not that she had ever tried to lure young men anywhere, but no-one would give her a second glance these days.

Mr Seligman couldn't believe that Aryanization would end with his company being liquidated. But when it happened, and the Nazis stole the business his family had created, he told them all to get out: to America, England, Australia – anywhere they had family. Saved their lives, really. Esther had chosen London, and cousins in Golders Green.

She'd found a job in the rag trade, though not at the level she'd reached at Seligman's. She kept trying to persuade the rest of the family to leave Berlin, every letter she wrote. The cousins gave her notes to enclose, offering a roof over their heads, introductions to employers, encouragement from the rabbi. They must be dead - it was over a year since she'd heard anything from Eva or Aunty Liane.

When she married Thomas, she had agreed to come down here to his family. It was hard leaving people who knew the old family stories, where you could talk German without being spat at. Thomas's folks tried their best to make her welcome, even though they looked at her as if she were a giraffe in the zoo. It wasn't a Jewish neighbourhood, and the family had assimilated, didn't keep any of the traditions. The atmosphere in the house was strained – polite, but everyone was very careful of what they said whenever Esther was in the room.

Thomas didn't really want her to work, and there were no fashion manufacturers worth approaching in Southampton. Her accent drew unwelcome comments when she tried the department stores, but she persevered, and found this factory job, making overalls and other workwear. A huge difference from the glamour of Leopold Seligman's, but gradually her colleagues started talking to her – especially when she revealed that she hated Hitler even more than they did.
Life was easier when she spent less time in the house. They had been happy for a couple of years, and had saved enough to start talking about getting a place of their own.

That was before Thomas was killed, with the rest of his family, in that air raid, back in September. She had been at work, and returned home to find a pile of rubble. She hadn't known what to do – a neighbour took her in for the night. But you had to pick yourself up, so she'd gone to work the next day, and a

Living in the past (and present)

colleague helped her find lodgings. So, you move on, and hope you hear the siren before the bombs start falling.

Susy Churchill

https://www.haaretz.com/israel-news/.premium.MAGAZINE-the-nazis-who-stripped-the-jewish-clothing-industry-bare-1.5931221

Life imitates Art

Extracts from a WW2 Diary.

As her only surviving relative, because my grandmother had
outlived my father, I had to fly red-eye into Southampton
straight after her death. Whilst clearing through her belongings
looking for her will, I discovered her diary. And stuck to the
front cover was an envelope addressed to me. Inside, in her
idiosyncratic writing, she stated that her dying wish was unusual,
but that she had marked the passages in her diary that would
explain everything. The passages had pink post-it notes and
were numbered in the order she wanted me to read them...

1)   October 4th 1940 My Mum didn't believe me when I
walked in the back door and told her that the Queen Mother's
niece had actually acknowledged my presence and said, "Thank
you, my dear," to me today.

2)   December 31ˢᵗ 1936 Today I handed in my notice. It's
goodbye to my first ever job. Farewell shop assistant at
Woolies. If war is coming, then I want to be "in it" rather than
just a stay-at-home. In order to qualify as a Voluntary Aid
Detachment worker (V.A.D to you and me) I've got to pass
First Aid exams and Home Nursing, plus do lots of hours
volunteering in the Royal Victoria Military Hospital. It's not that
far to walk from our house in Woolston.

3)   August 30ᵗʰ 1939 Like most people this year I never for a
moment expected war to suddenly be so near. It is now
apparent that I was wrong – I am determined not to be left out
of it all.

4)   September 15ᵗʰ 1939 I was 'called up' today and I'm now in
Number 4 Company Royal Army Medical Corps at... can you
guess where? Yes. Dear old R.V.M.H !

5)   September 16th 1939 What a dump! The Hospital now seems more dour and uninviting than ever. We have our quarters in what were the old barrack rooms and an outside lavatory on the balcony and cold water from the taps with tin basins.

6)   September 19th 1940 Yesterday the cookhouse was told to send a churn of hot water up to the balcony for us, which was better, but today we complained at the greasy hot water and on further investigation it was found that the kitchen had lost a churn of beef tea!

A group of uniformed women including VADs outside Netley Hospital, Southampton
HRO: 92M91/69/4

7)   September 21st 1940 In my experience, sad to say, most of the patients aren't very nice to us. They only want to talk about themselves. It is understandable those with amputations would feel sorry for themselves and need to grieve. But nearly all of them are unable to show any interest in our lives. They are incapable of asking about us and how we feel about our brothers at the front. In fairness it seems that hospitals

infantilise patients and military hospitals particularly so. It is military discipline throughout, which frankly Staff Nurse with her triplicate forms seems to relish.

It nearly broke my heart when one corporal the night before being sent back whispered that he didn't want to die a virgin. Most of the time the squaddies were thankful, or so they said, for our apparent cheerfulness. However, there was one of the longer stay patients that asked about me and my life. He has started calling me 'Beefy'. You can guess why! At first I felt insulted, but he has such a twinkle in his eye when he calls me over that it's becoming difficult to be as professional with him as I would wish. Perhaps I shouldn't, but now I'm calling him 'Marmite'.

7)   September 28th 1940 Today Staff Nurse lectured all 6 of us V.A.D.s about keeping our distance from the patients, and when she said about not having any favourites I fancied that she was looking straight at me. I thought at first it was because our group is moving to night shifts from tomorrow. But the gossip is that the Staff Nurse on the next ward has been sacked just for becoming pregnant. She's been kicked out of the staff accommodation and rumour has it that the father is one of the patients.

8)   October 1st 1940 Last night was the most frightening of my life. None of the patients could sleep a wink. The Nazi bombers kept flying over us from dusk to dawn. I should have spent the whole 12-hour shift going from bed to bed checking that every patient was OK. But the truth of the matter is that it was patient 'Marmite' that had to spend a lot of time keeping, as he put it, 'his Beefy Bovril' calm enough to keep on working and not hiding under the bed as apparently one of the VADs in the next ward did. To cap it all 'Marmite' told me he was being discharged on the 3rd and returning to active service. He asked if he could 'walk out' with me and without thinking I said "Yes".

9) October 2nd 1940 The news from Southampton is terrible. One house in Mum's street was bombed, but Mum is as OK as she can be. The one thing that is keeping me going is looking forward to seeing 'Marmite' when he's no longer a patient and I'm not bound by what Staff Nurse says.

10) October 3rd 1940 'Marmite' and me were on our way to the Red Lion in the High Street. We were stepping carefully through the rubble outside the remains of Holyrood Church when we heard singing. We couldn't resist peeping through the broken stained glass window and a wedding was actually taking place. 'Marmite' whispered "Perfect" and insisted that we enter and stand at the side. As soon as the wedding was over he goes down on one knee and proffers what looked suspiciously like a curtain ring and asks me to marry him! Well I was dumbfounded, so he tells me that the other patients love having the Queen Mother's niece to "royally" look after them, but to him I'm his royalty.

11) April 21st 2019 It was my 'Marmite's' dying wish that his ashes be discreetly scattered inside the shell of Holyrood at the spot where we were standing when the photograph that appeared in the local paper was taken. It is my dying wish that my ashes join him there.

Peter Nicol-Harper

Evacuation

Wednesday, 26 July, 1939
HOORAH! We have broken up. No more school until 4
September. I have worked SO hard this term and I hope
mummy and daddy are pleased with my report. I even managed
a B in Latin which is not my good subject. I am planning to (a)
stay in bed late every morning, (b) visit Cynthia, (c) play with Mr
Snuffles, my guinea pig, (d) take Miggy for walks and (e) possibly
help mummy. I am not going to do anything with Daphne
because even though she is my sister she's only eleven and too
childish to spend time with. I am only interested in mixing with
mature people, like Cynthia.

Thursday, 27 July.
A gloomy and very frightening day. After tea, mummy and daddy
took us into the drawing room and asked us to sit down, so I
knew it was serious. I could see daddy had my report envelope
in his hand so I thought I was in trouble but he pulled out a
leaflet which said that if war came, Daphne and I would have to
be evacuated. I told him we thought war was coming last year
and it didn't so wouldn't this be the same and he said no,
because Hitler was already advancing across Europe. I asked him
why we couldn't stay at home and he said Southampton might
not be safe because of the docks, and because he was a doctor,
he would be needed if people were injured. Daphne started to
cry and I wanted to but daddy said we would have to be brave
and children all over Europe were in a far worse position than
we were.
The leaflet told us all the things we'd need to take with us and
said we should keep a case packed and ready. Mummy read it
and said she thought it was disgraceful that girls could only take
one spare pair of knickers; she insisted that Daphne and I took
four each. Daphne got upset in case that meant there wouldn't
be room for Growler. I told her I'd take her spare knickers so
she could fit Growler in with her other stuff. I certainly didn't

want to get caught with a teddy in my luggage. Mummy said we should put everything into our backpacks to leave our hands free as we'd have lots of other stuff to take as well.

After that I went to Cynthia's and we both agreed it was the most frightful thing, especially as we didn't even know where they would send us. It might be Wales or Scotland but wherever it was, we hoped we'd be close to each other. Her mum had made a chocolate cake and it was delicious. Cynthia ate two slices but I only ate one to be polite.

Saturday, 29 July.
We are on holiday on the Isle of Wight! We had one scary moment when daddy said he would cancel our holiday this year but mummy said it might be our last chance for a long time and we would just go for a week and not a fortnight. However, I am v v cross because I still have to wear a knitted bathing costume and not a grown up one and when it gets wet it slips down and shows my chest which can be v embarrassing when I come out of the sea. I shall have to be careful that there are no boys around when I go for a swim, as I don't want them looking at me.

Wednesday, 2 August.
This is bliss and I am getting a suntan. Daphne is being a nuisance as she wants me to play with her but I don't want to make sandcastles any more. I am far too old for that kind of thing. She needs to understand that I am 14 and not interested in children's stuff. I can't believe we're half-way through our holiday already.

Saturday, 5 August
Back home, rotten luck. While we were away, a leaflet arrived saying, 'When the air raid warning goes, What shall we do?' Daddy read it then gave it to mummy who said there was nothing to worry about but that they would get a shelter for the garden. Then they told us there was going to be a black-out

exercise, during the night on Wednesday. Daphne asked if they would drop bombs to make it real and I told her not to be such a clot although I wasn't entirely sure what was going to happen. Daddy has been very busy. All children have to be vaccinated against diphtheria before they can be evacuated and so many parents haven't bothered to get this done they are bringing them all to his surgery now.

Thursday, 10 August.
V tired today. Between midnight and four o'clock in the morning, we had the blackout exercise. Everyone had to make sure they didn't show any lights from their homes, which was easy for us as we were all in bed by then and wouldn't have noticed, only the sirens went off and woke us up TWICE! This was at midnight and again at two o'clock. It was very frightening. Daphne came and climbed into my bed, bringing Growler with her. She hadn't cut her toenails which were v sharp so I told her off but actually I was a bit frightened myself so was glad she was with me, apart from the toenails which she kept digging into my shins. I shall have to mention this to mummy.
Later
Told mummy about Daphne's toenails and mummy said she'd cut them after Daphne's bath. Daphne got very cross and called me a snitch which wasn't fair because they were so long I don't know how she could have got her feet into her shoes.

Saturday, 12 August
Mummy took us to Plummers for our school uniforms. I didn't need much but Daphne is starting at the Grammar School in September so she will need a new velour hat, beret, tie, scarf, blouses and gym slips. We didn't have to get so many gym slips and blouses because she can wear my old ones. She was very cross about this and said she wanted new ones but Mummy said it was wrong to waste good clothing, especially with a war coming. Daphne will have my old gabardine and I will have a new one. Then we went to French's for our new school shoes

(hideous), wellingtons and slippers. I saw some really pretty red shoes with a slight high heel and I asked mummy if I could have those instead of my school shoes and she said absolutely not because they weren't school regulation and besides I would never go anywhere else where I could wear them. I said how could I go anywhere nice if I didn't have decent shoes to wear. She told me not to shout which I thought was wrong because I had used a perfectly sensible and calm voice, and when we got home she sent me straight to my room. IF I ever have any children I will let them have just the shoes they want. After all, it is their feet.

Monday, 14 August
WE ARE TO BE EVACUATED. Daddy brought the paper home with him and it said the Grammar School girls will be sent to Bournemouth. All the children in Southampton will be sent to seaside resorts along the south coast but I am glad we have Bournemouth because it isn't too far from home. We will be there from the beginning of term.
I went to Cynthia's after tea and she is like me. She is a bit scared and a bit excited. We are hoping we will be living close together but are sad because we cannot take our dogs with us.

Wednesday, 16 August
Really bad news today. Daddy has arranged for Daphne and me to stay with Dr and Mrs McFarlane, friends of theirs in Bournemouth when we are evacuated. Daddy met him when he was working as a doctor in the Great War but he is even older. He and his wife are at least fifty!!! I thought we would stay in a school, like the Chalet School in the books, but without the skiing. Now we are just going to have to spend it being kind to old people. We have visited them twice before. They have two sons but one has just finished at Cambridge and the other is at medical school so they won't be there. It is going to be awful.

Living in the past (and present)

Saturday, 19 August
Really bad day today. I asked mummy if I could have my hair permed before we went to Bournemouth and she said absolutely not without even considering it from my point of view which I do not understand because my hair is just like hers, straight as pump water. I asked her why not and she said that only a particular kind of girl had her hair permed, whatever that may mean. I told her Beryl Page at school had a perm and mummy just said, 'Exactly.'

Tuesday, 22 August
Not long now until the beginning of term. Daphne says she is feeling sad because she won't be seeing her old friends and she won't even be starting at the Grammar School near us. I told her not to be such a chump because some of her friends will be going with her and we will be living at the seaside. I also told her that I would look after her which I don't really want to do because she can be very babyish at times and I don't want my friends noticing.

Thursday, 24 August
More news on our evacuation. We are going to leave on Saturday, 2 September. Honestly, if it wasn't bad enough going back to school in the first place, they are making us go in on Saturday. Everyone on the other side of the Itchen is being evacuated on Friday, lucky them. Supposing war starts on Friday night, what will happen to us and we are losing a day of our holiday as well.

Saturday, 26 August
Mummy told us at breakfast this morning that she will be travelling to Bournemouth on Saturday too. They are laying on buses for blind people, cripples and ladies who are going to have babies. Because mummy used to be a midwife, she will be travelling with them. She said she'd bring more clothes for us as

we wouldn't be able to carry all the clothes we needed. I said I hoped none of the ladies would have their babies on the bus and mummy said she hoped so too although I wasn't entirely sure what happens when you have a baby but I want mummy to think I am grown up so maybe she will let me have a perm at Christmas.

Friday, 1 September
Last full day at home. Who knows where we will be this time tomorrow. We have hardly seen daddy since we got back from the Isle of Wight because he has been so busy. I hope they will look after Miggy and Mr Snuffles. I have written instructions for them on how to look after Mr Snuffles while I am away. I think they know how to look after Miggy but I have reminded mummy that he needs to go for walks twice a day. Mummy did a really special tea with cake, scones and even cream and strawberry jam.
We have to go to bed early tonight because we have to be at school at HALF PAST SIX tomorrow morning, which I think is quite ridiculous.

Saturday, 2 September
So much to write about today. We got up at half past five and put on our school uniforms. Daphne grumbled because she said hers was itchy and she started to cry but I think she was crying because she was frightened so I put my arms around her and told her she would stop itching soon.
We both had labels with our names and addresses tied onto our coat buttons. I felt like a little child but Daphne said it made her feel like a parcel and she was going to post herself to Bournemouth, which cheered her up a bit. Mummy had made egg sandwiches and little packets of nuts and raisins. She'd put some water biscuits and cheese into another bag and gave us an apple each. She also put a bag of barley sugar sweets into each of our back packs then checked we were both carrying our gas masks.

Living in the past (and present)

Daddy and Mummy weren't allowed to come to school to say
goodbye, but they walked with us to the corner of the road.
Our auntie lives near and she came to say goodbye as well and
gave us some more barley sugar. Daddy said she was very
naughty but winked. They hugged us and said goodbye and
mummy's voice was a bit wobbly. Then we walked off but every
time I looked back, they were still standing there, watching us
and waving, until we were out of sight.
At school we all had to go to our form rooms from last term
and everyone was shouting with excitement. Cynthia looked a
bit scared as she didn't know where she'd be that night. Daphne
looked a bit lost and I thought she was going to blub again but
all my friends crowded round her, saying, 'Isn't she sweet,' and
'Don't worry, we'll look after you'. I didn't tell them that in the
summer holidays I'd caught her walking down the road with Mr
Snuffles in her dolls' pram, all dressed up in dolls' clothes.
Beryl Page was there and her perm has started to grow out. It
is flat on top and frizzy at the ends and does not look good so
just for once mummy may have been right. I will not mention it
at Christmas.
Miss Bromhead, came in wearing an armband, and everybody
stopped shouting. She read a list of all our names and then gave
each of us a railway ticket and a postcard we could send to our
parents when we arrived although we would not need this.
Then we were all given a special number and were told the
same number would be given to our parents, so if anything
happened, we'd all be able to find each other again. I don't think
Daphne really understood what that meant because she was
just looking round the classroom with her mouth open. Then
Miss B told us we'd set off to walk to the station at 10 o'clock
but as it was still only half past seven it seemed ridiculous that
we had to be at school that early. Some girls were already
starting their lunch but Miss B told them to stop because they
didn't know when they'd be eating again.
Then we all went to the hall for a special assembly and Miss
Platford our head told us we were to be ambassadresses for the

Girls Grammar and not just Southampton and that we should always behave with bravery and decorum and not let the school down, our parents down or ourselves down. Then we sang Praise my soul the King of Heaven and all went back to our form rooms.

At 10'o'clock we all lined up in the grounds and then set off for the station in a crocodile. Our games mistress, Miss Westmacott, walked in front with a sign on a pole, saying Girls' Grammar School. It was really hot because we wore our gabardines rather than carrying them as we had so much other stuff. We had to take all our school books as well. After about a mile, Daphne began to grumble saying her new shoes hurt her. I told her it wouldn't be long before we reached the station and thank goodness we saw it soon after that otherwise she would have grumbled even more. I was also v relieved because it would have been very embarrassing if she had cried in front of my friends.

Tauntons' boys were already there and some of the older girls started giggling and waving until Miss Westmacott told them to start behaving like ladies. It was silly that we had arrived at the station so early because we had to wait another half an hour for the train. We were either walking a lot or waiting around so I was glad when the train arrived.

So much has happened. When we got to Bournemouth they made us walk to the school and it was nearly three miles from the station!!! It was half past one when we got there and they said we could eat our lunches but a lot of girls had eaten them already. They then matched the girls with the people they were staying with. That must have been very scary for some of them and despite Dr and Mrs McFarlane being old, I was quite relieved that we sort of knew them.

I thought I recognised Dr McFarlane and I was right because he saw us and went up to Miss Bromhead and showed him a letter which I think daddy had sent him and Miss Bromhead nodded and called us out. I was so pleased it was him because we were so tired by then. Even better, he had come to fetch us in his car so we didn't have to walk any more.

Their house is quite near school and is a bit like ours. It has four bedrooms and one was their son, Donald's but it's quite big so Mrs McFarlane asked if Daphne and I would mind sharing as Donald would give it up for us and sleep in the boxroom when he came home.

It is actually a very pretty room with a window onto the back garden. There are two beds, two chests of drawers and one wardrobe. It even has its own washbasin. We each chose a different bed, thank goodness and I drew a line across the carpet with my foot and told Daphne she is not to come over it with her mess.

The best thing is they have a dog. He is a West Highland terrier called Hamish and Dr McFarlane got him because he is Scottish himself so I imagine Hamish makes him feel at home.

Mrs McFarlane had made a cottage pie for dinner. Just as we were about to sit down and eat it, mummy arrived. We were so pleased to see her and wanted to show her our room but Mrs McFarlane said we could show her after we'd eaten.

Fortunately, none of the ladies had their babies on the bus and mummy was also able to bring a huge bag with more of our things.

Judy Theobald

The Windrush Generation

Our group saw a photo of the "Windrush Generation" arriving at Southampton docks. We knew that HMS Windrush didn't ever dock in Southampton, but that the HMS Almanzora certainly did. This section of writing is both historical and modern, because of the recent publicity about the present Windrush scandal.

Southampton's Windrush memorial mural at St. Mary's Fire Station

Generation Almanzora Still Sitting in Limbo

16/6/2020

Dear Prime Minister

I, as a grandchild of the Windrush Generation, am writing this letter to get to you before the 22nd of June the day your Government has designated as the first Annual Windrush Day. I am sending a copy of this letter to the Southern Daily Echo and the Guardian.

My grandfather arrived at Southampton Docks aboard the HMS Almanzora on the 21st of December 1947. He was ex RAF, but not one of the stowaways that were imprisoned for 28 days the next day. In 1963 he paid for my mother and me aged 4 to join him in Southampton. I arrived on Mama's Grenadian passport as a British subject. As you will know the 1971 Immigration Act guaranteed the right of those already settled in the United Kingdom to remain indefinitely.

You won't be able to imagine my shock when in 2013 I received a letter from the UK Border Agency telling me that I was required to leave the UK, as I no longer had a right to remain. That was frightening enough, but then despite being employed at Southampton's General Hospital all my working life, my contract was suddenly not renewed. I was later denied my radiotherapy despite paying taxes for decades. I was told I could go Private if I paid £54,000. The following year when I became unable to pay the rent I ended up in a homeless hostel because, and I quote "The Government does not fund Bed and Breakfast places for Illegal immigrants". I was frightened to see the Home Office vehicles with Immigration Enforcement written on the side and a picture of handcuffs saying "Go home or face arrest". But where was my home? I had no memory of Grenada and no living relatives there.

Living in the past (and present)

I was unable to get proof from Southampton Council that I had entered the UK legally because the Landing Card Slips had been destroyed by the Home Office in 2010. Over the next six months I built up a file of 75 pages containing my St Marys Primary School reports, tax details, bank statements, doctor and dental records and copies of the twelve letters that I had sent to the Border Agency. It gradually became obvious to me that they were not even bothering to read anything from me because they were only interested in fulfilling their quotas and no more.

I began to wonder if I had done something terribly wrong in my previous life. I felt ashamed and lost confidence in going to my own church. I was lonely, depressed, exhausted, humiliated, stressed and fearful of every knock on the door. I felt de-humanized. I considered taking an overdose. There seemed to be only one way of avoiding the terrifying deportation in handcuffs. Acting on auto pilot I applied for self-deportation whereby the Government would pay my one-way flight to Grenada. I naively still hoped for a last-minute reprieve, but that just meant that I had to throw mostly the wrong things into my bags. For all my worldly goods I was restricted to only a 20 kilo baggage allowance.

In Grenada I was 4,300 miles from the place that I had always regarded as my home. My English accent when I tried to introduce myself to the local church meant that they thought that I was a 'deported criminal'. I struggled to get used to the food and the climate.

You, Prime Minister, may feel that after the Windrush Scandal was revealed by your sister-in-law the Guardian journalist, that paying for my ticket back has sorted the matter. But I have returned to nothing. I have been rehoused in an unfurnished tiny flat in Millbrook far from my relatives and with no entitlement to a furniture grant. I'm 59 years old and I have to start rebuilding my life from scratch. Before this I felt British. I just did. I'm the sort of person who would watch every Royal wedding on TV. I feel less British now. I feel I don't belong here and I don't belong in Grenada either. I'm still looking over my shoulder all the time. I'm a nervous wreck.

There is still a sense of the 'hostile environment' continuing, for example, as recently as this February. I admit that my nephew committed a minor offence, but he was one of 25 out of 42 from Colnebrook and Harmondsworth Detention Centre who weren't deported - only because it didn't have a working mobile phone signal for them to access legal advice. You and your government were going to deport him anyway.

The specific reason for writing to you is to ask when is my compensation going to arrive? My request for urgent support has been denied. I know that two years on only 60 out of 1,275 had received compensation.
Is your government aware that with climate change set to displace approximately 1 billion people by 2050, surely questioning barriers to immigration is more necessary now than ever?

Two years ago my MP stated in Parliament "The government in Whitehall thought that this was a group of people that really didn't matter".
Black Lives Mattered Then, Matter Now and Will Do So Forevermore, Amen.

Yours

Peter Nicol-Harper

Living in the past (and present)

WIndrush (A young man's thoughts on arrival)

I know what I can do
I know what I can achieve

But can I be successful here
Will they recognise my worth
Do they see a black face
and assume ignorance?

They shun me in the classroom
Step sideways on the streets.
Where is the promised welcome
The vibrancy, the joy?

Here my mother's food lacks love and soul
Father's suits hang loosely on his diminished frame.
I try to buoy them up.

I have the youth
I have a power a strength within
We will survive, we will succeed.

Val Claisse

No Sympathy for the Devil

"Be not inhospitable to strangers, lest they be angels in disguise"

Please allow me to introduce myself.........

I began my life in 1930 in Hamburg when I was registered by the name of Rosa. My parents were both Jews, Blohm and Voss. I was named Monte Rosa but I always thought of myself as Rosa.

As a toddler I sailed with lots of Germans to South America many times and especially to Argentina.
From the age of nine I was taught that the British were my enemy.
Aged 10 'Strength through Joy' sent me to Norway.
Just before I became a teenager I helped transport 46 bad people from Oslo. I overheard that they were bound for a place called Auschwitz.
Aged 14, I assisted in taking Norwegian women who had been impregnated by the occupying Fascists to Germany.

Pleased to meet you, hope you guess my name

In 1945 I was abducted by British men in uniform who insisted on giving me a new name.
As an adult......

I stuck around

India when it was partitioned.
And I was there helping to fight the Communists in Korea.
I died on the 24th of March 1954 and was buried at sea. My grave is 37 degrees North and 2 degrees East.
There was an Inquiry into my untimely death (and a whitewash).

Living in the past (and present)

There was one really good thing that I did in my life and that
was in June 1948, when at the request of the British
Government I brought 500 good people from Kingston, Jamaica
to Tilbury Docks - and I'm pleased that I'll be always
remembered for it.

Pleased to meet you. Hope you guess my name.

You'll know me better by my British name
Win D Rush (With or Without the Empire)
PS I hear a rumour that there may be a second Government
Inquiry about me. I hope that this time it won't be another
whitewash.

Peter Nicol-Harper

Romanies

Travellers and Romany People
When considering the migrant population in Southampton City, one
could not disregard the Romany community, who have been visiting
Southampton seasonally for centuries. They have contributed their skills
and labour to its economy, and their unique lifestyle has made its
history colourful.
Our inspiration for writing creative stories about the Romany
community largely came from internet sources and from personal
recollections.

Romany children in the New Forest

Always on the Move

It is a glorious summer morning, birds are chirping outside and the sun has just started to rise from the edge of the world. With a cup of tea at my elbow, I sit to continue writing my memoirs. If my parents were alive, they would not approve of what I am going to write about now.

When they first told me of our Romany origin, I was about ten. "Don't tell anyone. I don't want you to be shunned," warned Dad, little knowing how his own prejudice had stirred my curiosity about my kith and kin, though his caution was comprehensible to me even at that age. Many Romany people who were in my story books were devious characters, drunkards, and they would steal, and would earn money by trickery, so I feared them. Their dirty-faced children generated aversion in me. Imagine my reluctance to admit my parents once lived with them! That night, when we went to bed, we were all equally exhausted, me with asking questions and them with their replies.

When the council had banned the Romany encampment in the New Forest, I was thirteen, and Dad took me to my Grandpa's trailer. Until then, I never knew my Grandpa was living there.

"This has been coming for years," said my father who was working in the docks. "People don't need horses to do farm work, now they have tractors and machines. Our people have to find work other than horse breeding and farm work. We have to change. Our children need a place in this world."

Grandpa protested, claiming that his people had been camping there for centuries, even before those councils were born. "These honest hands can find work anywhere I live," he said, looking at his outstretched hands. "I'm too old to change," he continued. "I will be going to Midlands next week. I can't stay put.

I'm always on the move." I still remember how he thrust his head back and laughed. That was the last I saw of him.

Mom had never gone to school, while Dad had stopped schooling when he was around nine years. Although he would turn out there clean and tidy, no one had come to play with him, or had shared his table at school. If something went missing from the classroom, at once, all the eyes, including the teacher's, had turned towards him. Even if the missing object was found later, they claimed he had put it back because of fear.

What made me an insatiable learner was my parents' inability to write and read and seeing how it shaped them and their lives. To make everything 'proper and legal' for me, they had registered their marriage, and they had been practising their signatures weeks before that, until those looked fitting on their marriage certificate!

"Going from one culture to another is harder than going from one moor to another," said Mom. When her parents were sent to the gas chambers in the 1940s, she was just four years old and had managed to escape to this country with another family.

Going camping on summer holidays was a tradition my parents kept for a long time even after I left home. In the evenings, in front of the campfire, he would play his fiddle while she would dance playing the tambourine.

My phone rings. Who could be ringing at this hour in the morning? The number of my son, who is working for a FTSE 100 company, appears on the screen.
"Hi Mom! Did I wake you up? I'm in Japan."
"Where? I thought you went to Hong Kong."
"Yes. That was last week. I will be flying to Rio de Janeiro next week. I'm working on a deal for our company. You know me,

Living in the past (and present)

Mom. I can't stay put. I'm always on the move." I hear him laugh and the echo of it rekindles my memory.

When did I last hear those exact words and that laugh?

Champika Wijayaweera

Caravans on the Common

The sky darkened, and I hurried outside to fetch in my laundry as the first fat raindrops started splattering the lawn. One after another, three brittle plastic clothes pegs disintegrated in my fingers, and I cursed our throwaway culture. There, at the end of the line, bleached by years of sunshine, the finely carved hazel peg sat tight. Where had all the others gone? For years my mother had bought the clothes pegs, strawberries and harvest plaits sold door to door by Mrs Cooper or one of her daughters. She would chat, asking whether Alice was married yet, or if Zeb's baby had arrived.

Ma argued with the neighbours, who tutted at her 'encouraging them thieving gyppos', but she and the Romany family who came calling twice a year had a long history. My mother came from farming stock in the New Forest, and Grandpa would choose the gypsy pickers whenever they were in the district: "Work dawn till dark, THEY will!" he declared – though not to all the villagers!

I was more cautious of the gypsies: Mrs Clark next door warned me not to go down to the Common when they were about: "Steal pretty little girls, they do – you'll never be seen again." Total nonsense, of course, but I believed it at the time. I wanted to fit in, be like everyone else. Ma had no worries about walking past their camp, and would pause to chat to travellers she recognised. I remember horses alongside their caravans when I was small, down on Weston Common, but there were motor vans by the late 1960s. I never had her ease in talking to them, though as a teenager, I was horrified to learn how Hitler had treated the Roma.

When had I last seen a gypsy hawker? A single recollection from Mayfield, where we lived for the first few years of married life, of a gypsy woman coming to the door. I had a baby on my hip, and a toddler was having a tantrum in his high chair. I was tired, and grumpy, having come to the conclusion that marriage and a family meant non-stop work. A trip to the shops was a major undertaking, and I missed the freedom of my single life. The Romany was selling clothes pegs, and I remembered Ma, decided I could stretch the housekeeping money, and bought a dozen. We chatted for a couple of minutes, and as she walked away, I would have traded places with her like a shot.

Susy Churchill

The 1901 census records five gypsy families camped at Weston Common, in the parish of St Marys Extra. At that time Weston Common stretched south from the A3024 to SE Road, and from Kathleen Road in the west to Butts Road in the east.

A traveller tale

Annie (not her real name) was a worldly-wise mature 8 year old. She lived with her parents and siblings on the local permanent Traveller site. She attended school very regularly, worked hard and was fascinated by 'living indoors,' in rooms of different shapes and sizes and with different uses; so unlike her trailer home.

She was the head teacher's obvious choice to show a visiting inspector round the school. A tour would normally take approximately 15 minutes. An hour later the head teacher was beginning to have misgivings about her choice of guide. Half an hour later Annie looking flushed with success delivered the exhausted inspector back to the office.

Tired but grinning widely he reported that it had been the most comprehensive and enjoyable tour of any school he had visited. It seems Annie had given him an in depth tour of every classroom including each teacher's competence to teach and the state of their store cupboards, many of which she confessed she would like to tidy up including her own class teacher's. Every toilet block was inspected and the boys' urinals came in for particular condemnation, 'stinking the place out,' in her parlance, her mum would be disgusted.

At the end of the day when the inspector was leaving he congratulated the head teacher on the confidence she placed in her pupils and he suggested she should put Annie on the school council as the child clearly had much of value to offer, particularly in how to keep a clean and tidy workplace. Suitably admonished the head teacher took his advice.

Val Claisse

(A true story from Val's teaching career)

Writing in the time of Covid

As a group creating writing inspired by archive material, it felt important that we produce our own contribution - for future writers? - on the experience of living through a global pandemic. We had investigated the lives of those who worked in the docks - which were now eerily silent. Reading stories of migration was even more poignant at a time when travel was severely restricted. Our lives were limited, but it was not the Blitz. What follows are some personal reflections.

30 July 2020: The writers gather, masked and socially distanced, in the remnants of Holyrood church, in their re-creation of the original wedding photograph.

Pandemic 2020

Coronavirus
an ambiguous illness
brought the world to heel

The progress
unknown
treatment, yet to
discover
it baffles science!

Paying silent gratitude to social media, I turned on the computer. A friend had posted an adorable family photograph of both husband and wife working from home while their two children were playing around them, with her comments about the bliss of lockdown. The entire social media website was dedicated to news of the virus, about unorthodox remedies for it, bizarre modes of transmission of it and multitude of graphs and maps which I skipped cheerily. Further down on the page, another friend had posted about the lonesome cremation of her cousin who died of coronavirus infection.

Alone lonely death
tied to a ventilator
funeral, denied

I left that website and started to read the online newspapers, in which everything seemed bleak. The need for a cup of tea was overwhelming, so I went to the kitchen. A few weeks before the lockdown, a supermarket range had offered complimentary seed pots for every twenty pounds that was spent in their stores, and I began to collect them because they came free. Neglected, they were on the kitchen worktop.

Usually, I don't enjoy gardening!

Living in the past (and present)

Perhaps, strange times change people's attitudes and their behaviour. I planted these seeds and watered them diligently. Thrilled with the sight of green shoots, I started to experiment with seeds from a tomato and a bell pepper which were at home.

The salad plants provided me leaves daily for almost two months. The carrots and beet plants grew beautifully with lots of foliage. So decorative! But the harvest below the ground was disappointing. There was a single beetroot about the size of a golf ball. That was all! But I made a tasty carrot leaf pesto once to go with home baked bread, and the rest of the carrot and beet leaves, I stir fried, and it was delicious with rice. I have no grouse about radish because that is not something I relish. I allowed them to grow, and their dainty pink and white flowers and trailing stalks have been making my hanging basket colourful. My chilli and tomato plants have just begun to flower. They will give fruits, I am sure they will.

Nature gives hope, hope of life!

Champika Wijayaweera

Living in the past (and present)

One day...

Twenty-four hours
Our world
Shrank.
Outside
became
Inside,
Nearness/Distance,
Joy/Grief,
Empowerment/Dependency.

Cautiously/Wiser?
We emerge,
Just three months later.

Val Claisse

Between the headlines

Items in Bold are headlines from the Southern Echo.
Items in italics are taken from my Google Activity log for the same date.

19th February
**Coronavirus racism reports spark 'extreme concern'
from Southampton uni chiefs**

*Searched areas around Galicia and Southern France and viewed details
of 30 holiday rentals (planning holiday with family). Read articles on
BBC news website: Amazon: How Bezos built his data machine;
Andrew Sabisky: No 10 adviser resigns over alleged race comments -
BBC News.*

27th February
**NHS staff at Southampton General Hospital 'being urged
to shave facial hair' over coronavirus fears**
*Loaded directions to Titchfield Festival Theatre (taking part in
'Hauntings' – their penultimate production before lockdown).Checked
Facebook twice. Articles on BBC website: UK weather: Snow and ice to
bring travel disruption - BBC News Coronavirus now spreading faster
outside China - BBC News . Booked crossings with Brittany Ferries.*

9th March
**Angry residents hit out at price of hand sanitisers in
Premier store, Bitterne Village**
*Posted on Facebook about taking part in Hauntings. Looked at plants
for sale from Haylofts Plants. Spent 10 minutes on Pinterest. Articles on
BBC website: Coronavirus symptoms: What are they and how do I
protect myself? - BBC News; Pixar's Onward 'banned by four Middle
East countries' over gay reference - BBC News. Played killer sudoku.
Checked weather forecast.*

29th March
Man arrested in Southampton for coughing in cars and saying he has coronavirus
Downloaded recipe for coconut bread. Scheduled Zoom meetings and emailed out links. BBC website articles: Machine translates brainwaves into sentences - BBC News; Coronavirus: Six things that are booming in sales - BBC News. Checked the spelling of 'epithalamion'. Looked at drawings my daughter posted on Facebook. Viewed schedule of Metropolitan Opera's free broadcasts.

11th April (Easter Saturday)
More than 200 who tested positive for coronavirus have died in Hampshire
Played Dominion and killer sudoku. Zoom call with our grandchildren. BBC News articles: Coronavirus: UK could be 'worst affected' country in Europe - BBC News; Coronavirus updates: Global fatalities near 100,000 - BBC News. Searched for online suppliers of compost. Visited Facebook. Searched for suppliers of delphinium plants. Half an hour on Pinterest.

21st April **Urgent appeal to help feed animals at Southampton City Farm**
Zoom meetings. Visited Southampton Libraries Borrowbox. Followed YouTube meditation. BBC articles: Coronavirus: Social restrictions 'to remain for rest of year' - BBC News. Zoom meetings. Read several articles on british-history.ac.uk. Watched opera 'Einstein on the beach'.

8th May **Southampton nurse thanked and handed award by Prime Minister**
Online banking. Zoom meetings. BBC articles: Supermoon lights up night skies around the world - BBC News, VE Day: UK's streets not empty as filled with love, says Queen - BBC News. Reviews of books on Amazon. Facebook. Pinterest.

18th May **PHOTOS: UK Freedom Movement protest at Southampton Common**

Ordered son's birthday presents from Amazon, Total Cards & Traidcraft – to be delivered to him. Zoom meetings. BBC: Coronavirus: Security flaws found in NHS contact-tracing app - BBC News, Downloaded Nigella recipe for 'sunshine soup'. Read article about the workhouse on seesouthampton.com

2nd June **Hampshire hospitals have again reported no new coronavirus deaths**

Zoom meetings. RHS Plant Finder. Downloaded directions to Southampton General Hospital after an accident in my garden.

23rd June **Flexible working requests expected to rise**

Zoom meetings. Downloaded recipes. Pinterest. Played Dominion. BBC: Jet2 and Eurostar cut summer flights and trains - BBC News; Sheffield pub where drinkers hid in cupboards loses licence - BBC News. Cancelled holiday booking. Submitted poem to Mslexia.

3rd July **Police 'preparing' for reopening of pubs across Hampshire this weekend**

Zoom meetings. Writers HQ course details. Good Housekeeping: dresses for summer. Searched Linkedin for treasurer for the charity I chair. Facebook. The Guardian: The Upside: The joy of missing out. BBC: Coronavirus in the South: Updates from 29 June to 5 July 2020 - BBC News.

15th July **Buzz Bingo in Antelope Park to permanently close**

Zoom meetings. BBC: Comet Neowise: How to spot incredible comet in the sky during July - CBBC Newsround, Summers could become 'too hot for humans'. YouTube meditation. Online banking. Downloaded recipes. Charity Commission. Signed 38Degrees petition.

Susy Churchill

Prompts and writing exercises

Poetry
We started the year by bringing in favourite poems and analysing them. Which lines resonated most? What did we enjoy about them?
We identified the importance of concrete imagery, rhythm and metre, the part the title plays, and how the sounds of words, whether guttural or slippery, can emphasise the meanings being communicated.

To develop our use of concrete imagery we did an exercise on 'Tools of the Trade': without naming the occupation, describe the actions taken, and/or tools used, in a normal day in your working life.

Visits
Galleries:
Who is the maker of this piece, or the character shown?
What do you imagine were their thoughts and feelings, hopes and fears?
What reactions are evoked in you?
What concrete images represent your felt experience?

Wedding among the rubble:
Prompted by a photograph of a wedding in a bombed church, with piles of rubble clearly visible:
Imagine yourself as one of the people attending this wedding - what thoughts and feelings are you experiencing? Why?

Living in the past (and present)

Neighbourhoods
Prompted by the article 'THE COUNTRY HOUSES OF
SOUTHAMPTON' By Jessica Vale,   Proceedings of Hampshire
Field Club Archaeological Society: 39, 1983, 171-190
Where were these houses?
What exists there now?
Geographical changes reflect social changes - a cause for nostalgia
or celebration?

Southampton in World War 2
Our starting points were photographs of Southampton during the
Blitz, the diary of Walter Kingston (Fire Warden), copies of the
Southampton Daily Echo, and other archive materials collated for
us by staff in the Local Studies team at Southampton Central
Library; supplemented by family records and material found
through internet searching.

What physical sensations would the people living through these
experiences have felt? Sights, sounds, smell, touch, taste?
Incorporate one or more physical sensations in your writing.

Life in the Workhouse
We studied resources collated by Peter Higginbotham, and
listened to oral histories of people who had lived in the children's
homes. From photographs, we imagined how children who had
grown up there would reflect on their lives.

Workhouses: Peter Higginbotham and
http://www.workhouses.org.uk/Southampton/

The Windrush Generation
Amongst the resources gathered for us by the lovely Local Studies
team at the Library were the book 'Windrush: The Irresistible

Living in the past (and present)

Rise of Multiracial Britain' by Mike and Trevor Phillips, and material on the previous lives of the 'Empire' ships. Back in the Seminar Room we did a 20 minute free writing exercise, drawing on our reading and the themes 'Fresh start/New beginnings' and 'Identities'.

Romanies
Continuing our theme of 'journeys' from the previous years, internet searching revealed the following:
New Forest Romany Gypsy Travellers: Stories
www.newforestromanygypsytraveller.co.uk
Census data: http://theromany.weebly.com/hampshire.html

Writing in the time of COVID
Becoming a virtual group, meeting through video-conferencing, threw us into individual internet searches for archive material to stimulate our writing. As we grew more comfortable with the medium we introduced a few more writing exercises:

From Natalie Goldberg's 'Writing Down the Bones':
'The Action of a Sentence' (P95-97)
Fold a piece of paper in half.
One per line, write a list of ten nouns (concrete things like 'table' or 'cat', rather than abstracts like 'justice').
Turn to the other side of the folded paper.
Think of an occupation, such as cleaner or mechanic.
List fifteen verbs, actions that someone in that occupation would do.
Open out the paper.
Combine a noun with one of the verbs in a sentence

Another exercise, from 'Finding Out' by Sara Maitland in 'The Creative Writing Coursebook', edited by Julia Bell and Paul Magrs:
Think of a fairy story, myth, or a story from a religious text
Tell the story from a different point of vie

Biographies

Richard Blakemore

Retired from a Civil Service career in 2014 Richard Blakemore was faced with no longer having the excuse of being too tired to do any creative writing other than the occasional poem and short story. Joining the So: Write Stories creative writing group has, through the use of archives and oral history, provided much imaginative stimulus and new direction thus weaning him away from his normal favourite subject: himself.

Following a family move from his birthplace of Bournemouth, Richard has now lived in Southampton for nearly sixty years, thus accumulating many memories both personal and of the changing city. One of the opportunities provided by the group's work is to attempt to weave personal memories together with past events and lives.

He studied social science at Southampton University during which time he married a born and bred Sotonian.

Susy Churchill

Susy is a psychotherapist, educator and author. Childhood journeying from County Durham through Nottingham, Malta, Cheltenham and Hertfordshire involved studying at seven different schools. Her work continued the trend, travelling through teaching, research and management consultancy.

Previously Programme Director of Counselling and Psychotherapy courses at the University of Southampton, her first publications were academic: 'The Troubled Mind' (Palgrave MacMillan, 2010), journal articles and conference presentations. Her flash fiction and poetry has appeared in Literary Orphans and Visual Verse. Other passions include gardening from a ladder at her hillside home and experimental cookery.

Valerie Claisse
Val spent forty years marking pupils and students' literary efforts but never really found the time to write anything of substance herself.
Retired now and determined to be 'a writer', she discovered to her chagrin that writing creatively was not as easy as she had fondly imagined. She also felt guilt and remorse about the amount of red pen she had scribbled over her students' scripts!
Val has really enjoyed learning with and alongside Nazneen and the other members in the writing group held at Southampton Central Library.

Lindsey Neve
I grew up between the villages of Warsash and Sarisbury Green, near to Southampton, part of a large, extended family. Leaving school at the age of 15, I worked in clerical and book-keeping roles and took various courses in accounting and business management, whilst also raising my family. In my thirties I joined the charity, the Jubilee Sailing Trust and worked there for 19 years, taking on the role of Chief Executive for the last 11 years of that time.
I have always enjoyed writing but only as a hobby. Much of my writing is centred around memories of my childhood. I became a member of the Netley Writers' Group in 2017 and very much enjoy being part of that stimulating, friendly group and also, briefly, of the Southampton Creative Histories group.

Peter Nicol-Harper
My full name is Peter Nicol-Harper. In "I make here become a home now" Anthology Number 1 (2018) the name I chose was Pete Nicol. (Was I after street cred?) In "Doors into History" Anthology Number 2 (2019) my name became Peter Nicol (Aspiring to be a slightly more mature writer?) In this Anthology Number 3 entitled "Living in the Past (and Present)" (2020) I have

chosen to write under my full name. Now like my name this Anthology contains an increased quantity of my writing (but hopefully some improved quality?)

This year we've changed the title of our Writing Group so, as I don't have any other first or second names, perhaps next year I will write under a 'nom de plume'?!

Becky Sharp

I have always loved books and especially making up my own stories. One of my earliest memories was coming up with my own version of Treasure Island because I loved the story so much but was disappointed that there were no main female characters. After all, why can't girls have adventures too?

Twenty years later I still love writing but I have also developed a love and passion for history. It was this love of history, which caused me to move to Southampton in 2010 to study for my MA. It also drives me with my job at Southampton City Council organising school visits to the city's museums and art gallery. My love for history stems from the same love of stories that I had as a child and provides inspiration for my writing now.

Judy Theobald

I spent much of my working life employed as a journalist in print and broadcasting so I've really enjoyed writing fiction, especially as we've based a lot of our short-story writing on facts discovered during our research. I've still used the disciplines of journalism, such as strict word counts and concise use of language, but it's been a pleasure to stretch my imagination to look beyond the bare bones of the story at what might also be happening in the background.

Champika Wijayaweera

Champika, a professionally trained doctor, anatomist and medical writer, has spent much of her time working in hospitals, lecture theatres and laboratories, so her initial writings were academic articles of her own research work. Now, she writes research papers for others. During the last decade, she has joined a couple of writing groups which have inspired her to write creatively. Her work has appeared in *The Sunday Observer*, Sri Lanka, and *Lakeview International Journal of Literature and Arts*.

Living in the past (and present)